IN SEARCH OF A MASTER

Other books by John Preston

Franny, the Queen of Provincetown
Mr. Benson
I Once Had a Master and Other Tales of Erotic Love
Entertainment for a Master
Love of a Master
The Heir

The Alex Kane Series:
Sweet Dreams
Golden Years
Deadly Lies
Stolen Moments
Secret Dangers
Lethal Silence
Classified Affairs
(with Frederick Brandt)
Safe Sex: The Ultimate Erotic Guide
(with Glenn Swann)
Hot Living! Erotic Stories about Safer Sex (Editor)

IN SEARCH OF A MASTER

JOHN PRESTON

KENSINGTON BOOKS
http://www.kensingtonbooks.com

KENSINGTON BOOKS are published by

Kensington Publishing Corp.
850 Third Avenue
New York, NY 10022

All Kensington titles, imprints and distributed lines are available at special quantity discounts for bulk purchases for sales promotion, premiums, fund-raising, educational or institutional use.

Special book excerpts or customized printings can also be created to fit specific needs. For details, write or phone the office of the Kensington Special Sales Manager: Kensington Publishing Corp., 850 Third Avenue, New York, NY 10022. Attn. Special Sales Department. Phone: 1-800-221-2647.

Kensington and the K logo Reg. U.S. Pat & TM Off.

ISBN 0-7582-0091-9

First Kensington Trade Paperback Printing: January, 2002
10 9 8 7 6 5 4 3 2 1

Printed in the United States of America

For Kevin, who conjures up such masterful dreams

Contents

IN SEARCH OF A MASTER

1

The Beginning

I didn't have to go in.

I turned and watched the car drive away. I could wave. I could run after him. I was sure he'd come back for me and that he'd understand. I watched the car accelerating. It disappeared around a corner. It was too late.

No, it wasn't! I could walk back, tracing the route we'd taken, and find a bus or a train at the town we'd passed through, not too far from here. It would only be a short walk on a pleasant summer day.

I didn't have to go through these gates and into that house. I looked at it. The building was an immense mansion. It was built of red brick. The grounds around it were impeccably maintained; the grass was evenly cut, and the hedges that lined the front path and others I could see around the property were all perfectly trimmed.

I was sweating from both the heat and the tension. I could feel the moisture running down from my armpits, over the sides of my belly. My underwear was damp. I could smell a sour odor from all of the perspiration.

I didn't have to go in. But what if I didn't? What would I go back to? A life working in a lumberyard in a mill town? Maybe a junior-college education if I disciplined myself enough to go through years of night school. A few clandestine meetings with strangers for sex? My hand pushed against the metal entry, and I walked through it. Once the gate clanged shut, it was done. I was here, and I wouldn't turn around.

I stood there for a short while. There was a wall that enclosed the whole area. It was brick. Just like the house. I suddenly felt some great relief to be surrounded by it. It was a definition of some sort of space. It told me that I could move, protected, within this area. I'd have rules I could understand and limits that could be seen easily. The wall meant something to me; it was much more important than rows of bricks.

Now I was a part of it, a confederacy that would separate me from the rest of the world. I belonged here now. I would belong. I was a part of the world that was defined, at least at this moment, by that wall. I only had to go into the mansion and I would be entering a final inner sanctum. I would be initiated.

I went up to the large front door. I held my finger out to push the button. Every step I'd made up the walk had seemed like another decision, but this was the largest of them all. If I rang this bell, I would be handing my body over to The Network for the next three years.

My finger moved toward the button and pushed. I breathed deeply, and my shoulders seemed to slump as though I needed to give all this a physical response.

I waited only for a short while. The blond man who answered wasn't much taller than I; I suspected he was six feet. He was much more heavily muscled, with broad shoulders and large, well-defined biceps that were clearly visible. He was wearing a T-shirt and shorts, both made of the same deep purple satiny material. He smirked at me but didn't say anything.

"I'm . . . I'm here for the sale," I finally stammered out. It seemed such a matter-of-fact statement. But I couldn't find other words, ones that could speak of the conspiracy I was entering.

He nodded. "Come this way."

I followed him through the wide corridors of the mansion. I could watch his muscles move under the fabric, especially his buttocks, which were pronounced pairs of flesh that rotated sexually as he walked. He led me into a small anteroom and waved a hand to one of the seats there. Only when I'd taken it did he go to the other door and knock very quietly.

A muffled voice answered. He went in and then returned in a very short time. "Mr. Cantrell will see you now."

I stood up and walked through this last portal, my stomach still tied in knots and my mind reeling. The door closed behind me. All I could think was: *There! I've done it. I don't have to decide anything more.* It felt as though some great burden had been lifted from me.

"Timothy, I'm pleased to meet you." The man who stood up behind the desk was much older than I had expected. But I immediately realized I had no right to any expectations in this affair. I walked over to him and took the hand he was holding out. He waved me into a straight-backed chair that faced him. He was white-haired, about sixty years old. He had very alive blue eyes and a deeply tanned face. He was a large man, another one who was about six feet tall. He was dressed in a dull-colored tweed sports coat with a brilliant yellow silk tie.

"I have your file here." He lifted up a portfolio and opened it. He read through some papers in it without saying anything more to me. I forced myself to watch the fireplace flames that were burning, even though it was warm out. The smell and sound made the office seem so deceptively cheery. Why would anyone have a fire at this time of year? I wondered vaguely, happy to have anything else to think about while Mr. Cantrell read.

"Yes, yes." He seemed to have satisfied himself about something. "Everything seems to be in order."

Then he looked up at me while he clasped his hands on top of the file, which he'd left open on the desk. He spoke as a doctor, one who was trying to convey his warmest friendship through an overpracticed manner and who would never convince you that his feelings were at all authentic.

"My role now, Timothy, is to make sure that you understand everything, *everything,* about the decision you will be making here today. Your contract with The Network runs for three years. That's not an inconsiderable length of time. I would be suspicious if I didn't know the man who's trained you. He supports your request with the belief that your interest in personal exploration is so great that you will be able to sustain such a long term of . . . slavery."

The last word hit hard. I hadn't heard it spoken out loud in weeks. I felt cold sweat coming out of my forehead. I moved in the chair and was immediately embarrassed that Mr. Cantrell would know just how horrible the word had sounded to me.

"You do still want to be sold on that basis, Timothy?"

"Yes, sir." I couldn't quite look him in the eye, and my voice was only half as loud as I knew it should have been.

"Very well. I do have to go over the particulars with you. It's one of our customs.

"We will assume that you will be sold this evening. That person—it will probably be a male, but there are women who attend our auctions—will provide The Network with an amount of money that will cover your contracted fee. This is the amount that you have determined is a worthwhile salary for three years of your life."

He looked down at the papers, and I was suddenly terrified that he was going to tell me that it was too much. But he said nothing more about it.

"You will belong—utterly—to the person who buys your

three years. You understand that you will have no rights whatsoever?"

"Yes, sir."

"Of course, the fundamental purpose of The Network is sexual pleasure, and that will certainly be the major reason for which you will be bought, but your owner has every right to demand physical labor of any sort and has no obligation to provide you with sexual favors at all."

"I understand, sir."

"I see here that you've met some who have already served in The Network. You probably have more knowledge of the possibilities than others might. That's to your advantage.

"Often people think—very erroneously—that all those who make purchases at The Network auction are very wealthy. But your trainer is only a moderately comfortable man, and you know that you might be sent to someone in his circumstances?"

"Yes, sir."

"The details." He closed the portfolio and smiled at me. "Your money will be deposited in monthly allotments in an interest-paying bank account in the Bahamas. When your time of service is up, you will be allowed to reconsider your options. You might choose to leave us, which is fine. There will be no attempt to hinder you. But you're only twenty-five, a good age to begin, neither too young nor too old. You will only be twenty-eight when this term is done, and you may well want to approach The Network for another sale—or your master for an extension.

"No coercion will be used to influence any of those decisions. I must warn you, though, that coercion will be used to hold you to this contract. We do maintain a system of surveillance that's astonishingly effective, Timothy. When a slave runs, we find him or her. Every time." The smile had disappeared from Mr. Cantrell's face. I could only nod now.

"This interview is given just before the auction as one

more step to make sure your judgment is clear and that you understand the situation perfectly. Now I must ask you to sign your contract as one last formality."

He reached across the desk and handed me a sheet of parchment paper. On it, written in fine calligraphy, was the statement that I had given myself up to The Network for sale for three years. I also imposed no restrictions other than those of the organization. He handed me a pen.

"You know that The Network's restrictions are extremely basic: Your owner may not permanently harm or mark you. You cannot be exposed to a preventable disease. But that is about all that is involved. Anything else is at your master's whim."

I took the pen and watched myself sign the contract. Cantrell reached over and took the document from me.

"Fine, then. I think we understand one another. The auction will be held here in my house this evening. My servants will prepare you." He reached down underneath his desk and seemed to push a button. The door opened, and the same scantily dressed man entered. "Take Timothy now."

My stomach was so tight with tension that I wasn't sure I'd be able to stand up, but I managed. When I had, Cantrell spoke again: "Timothy, you'll have no more need for those clothes. Take them off."

I had very little on; I had been warned about that. I slipped the polo shirt over my head and stood stripped to the waist. I bent down and pulled off my loafers and socks. Then I stood again and unzipped my pants. I pulled my slacks and my underwear down over my legs. The smell of nervousness was more intense now that there weren't clothes to cover it up.

The servant reached over and took the clothing from my hands and picked up the things I'd left on the floor. He walked over and put them in the fireplace. I watched the flames begin to consume them.

Cantrell had come around to the front of the desk. He

stood in front of me and seemed to be judging my body. I could feel my cock lift up in erection at the idea of being there, naked, having this stranger evaluate me. I knew what he saw.

I was well built, trim, not really developed the way the other man in the room was. I had a thick covering of hair on my chest but none on my belly. It wasn't until my pubic area that my body hair flared out again. My cock was decent-sized. My balls were tight, smaller than you'd expect to go with my penis. My legs were my best feature, especially my thighs. In another time and in another place I might be very happy with my attributes. But now they seemed so minor, insignificant.

This wasn't a bar where I and other men were judging each other on at least somewhat equal terms. This wasn't a beach where we were only vaguely gauging each other's appearance. This was the beginning of The Network, and this was the first master to consider me.

The servant was moving behind me. He grabbed my hands and began to put on leather restraints to bind them together.

Cantrell walked back to sit behind his desk and picked up some papers. As he began to read them, he said, "You will do." Then the servant dragged on my hands and pulled me out the doorway.

2

Andre

I walked behind him through the corridors of the house. I was naked, my cock half-hard and swinging from side to side, humiliating evidence of how I was reacting to this scene.

The place felt more like a museum than a house. The rooms didn't seem to be really designed to be lived in. I didn't see any other people until we came across two men who were dressed in the same outfit as the first servant. They were hard at work moving pieces of furniture around in what appeared to be the largest room of all. They paid no attention as we passed through. My nakedness wasn't even worth noticing to them. It made the humiliation more intense to realize that I was so conscious of being nude when no one else cared.

My guide led me through a swinging door, and we were suddenly in another part of the house. The wood paneling ended; in its place were white painted walls. The floors were no longer parquet; they were simple linoleum. The man in the purple satin stopped suddenly and turned to take hold of my upper arm. He stared at me for a moment. It was a withering look, half contempt, half pity.

"They like to do things like that to you," he said. I didn't understand at first, but he continued: "Things like burning your clothes in front of you. It's one of their little ways to let you know from the beginning that you've lost it all by coming here."

That was all he said. I couldn't get any words out in time to ask him more. I wanted to; that was certain. I thought I had asked all the questions there could be before I got here, but now there were so many more, and they seemed so much more urgent. And whatever else I thought about how he was treating me, the fact that he'd tried to explain that one thing meant something to me. I was overwhelmingly thankful that he'd given me that information; I wanted to tell him that.

But before I could say anything, he used his grip on my arm to propel me through another door.

The room was full of activity. There was another man whom I took to be one of Mr. Cantrell's servants. He had on only a pair of shorts; they were the same purple color. He was standing in front of a very handsome, light-skinned black man. In a row, parallel to the first nude male, were four others: two men and two women. All of them were naked.

I knew these were the others who'd be sold tonight. I could tell because I could see on their faces the same disbelief that I knew had to be on my own. I could also sense the same terror growing in them that was beginning to churn inside me.

"Peter, is this the last one?" the servant asked when he saw we had arrived. *Peter!* At least I had a name for him.

"Yes. There was another, but he canceled at the last minute." Peter was taking the cuffs off my wrists. I barely noticed. I was too pleased—actually, I was proud to know I'd gone through this and someone else had failed. In the middle of it all, I clung to that small bit of confidence. My indecision at the gate was a rapidly fading memory. Peter nudged me toward the line, and I stood by the black man and tried to take in the details of the room and all that was happening around me.

There was no furniture, only a line of lockers along one

wall. Behind me was a line of very wide shelves covered by flat pillows. Off to the side was a shower area. In between were a pair of urinals and two open, unprotected toilets.

Except for the rough canvas-covered mats on the shelves, the entire room was covered with white tile, floor and ceiling as well as walls. I suddenly realized that this was the place where the house slaves lived. I had a rush of fear when that recognition hit me. I looked around and saw how totally devoid of privacy and personal space their lives were. The shelves were their beds, but there was no hint of a partition or of a single individual touch. They'd even be open to view when they used the toilets.

"Listen up," Peter said loudly to get our attention. "This is what will be happening. You're going to get a rest right now and, later, some food. Relax—as much as you can. In a few hours we'll come back and prepare you for the auction. It takes place at midnight. You'll be on display for two hours before then.

"Talk to one another if you want; no one will be bothering you. When we come back, we aren't going to harm you or do anything that you need to worry about. The men are going to get shaves; all of you will be cleaned up.

"Do you have any questions?" He looked up and down the line. When no one spoke, he and the other man left.

The six of us were left alone in the room. One couple—a male and a female—obviously were together and moved immediately to hold on to each other. They went to a corner where the woman seemed to be comforting the man. The other woman went over to the shelves and sat down, looking forlornly out the window, her legs drawn up under herself.

The other two men and I stood there and awkwardly glanced at one another. We nodded first; they must have been just as unsure of their right to speak as I was. We all stupidly tried to cover our genitals, as if we had suddenly rediscovered our modesty.

"I'm Tim," I finally said.

"Andre," the beautiful black man responded.

"And Glen," the third one said.

We moved to an unoccupied corner and took seats on the shelves. I ran a hand over the surface. There was only a slight cushion, something like a Japanese futon. There wasn't even a blanket. I realized that the main part of the house had been air-conditioned; I'd been chilled when I'd walked through it without any clothing. But this room was actually very warm.

Stripping in front of Cantrell hadn't been this devastating to me. I was now looking at how I might be living my life for the next three years.

"Scared?" Glen asked, perhaps reading my mind.

I nodded.

"I'm terrified." Andre answered the same question. But he smiled when he said it, as though it weren't a state he minded being in. His skin was the color of light café au lait. There was no hair on his chest at all and only a little bit on his legs. His muscles were perfect: Some were perhaps a little exaggerated—his biceps, his ass, and his pectorals were too large for the rest of his frame—but even that made him seem more sexually appealing.

He had a full head of curly black hair. His thick eyebrows were matched by a full mustache. There wasn't a blemish anyplace on his body, not one.

His cock and balls fascinated me. He seemed to still be half-erect—so was I—which made me more aware of the darker-colored skin of his genitals. The balls were bigger than mine, and the uncircumcised cock was as large as my own.

Glen obviously didn't want to talk. He sprawled out on his back next to us. Glen was also handsome; there was no doubt about that. But his looks were totally different from mine or, certainly, Andre's. He was very blond, with almost no body hair, clean-shaven, with a torso like my own: trim, tapered. He could have been any model in a men's clothing catalog; he was just as perfect. Just as bland. The exotic look of Andre's coffee-colored skin interested me much more than anything about Glen.

We sat there silently for a long time. I let the idea of Andre's attractiveness take over my mind. I welcomed anything that helped keep me from thinking about what I had done—what we were doing. But the topic was too present for Andre as well as me.

"How did you get here?" he finally asked me.

I didn't mean to avoid his question, but I honestly didn't know how to stop my confusion long enough to figure out a starting point. He waited, obviously wanting me to be the one who began. I struggled to do it, hoping that forcing myself to form words might give this whole experience some coherence:

"I come from a small town in New England, not too far from here. Everything about it is . . . boring. I was married when I was very young, but that wasn't real. That was just me trying to fool myself. I went into the service to get away. But I only lasted for two years. After I got out, I did odd jobs.

"While I was away in the service, this man had moved into town. I had a friend who was still at home—someone I used to fool around with—and they got to know each other. When I got out of the military, I met this man, too. He never really invited us to do anything with him, but he let us in on what was going on in his life.

"It was this stuff." I couldn't seem to put a name to it. "I was . . . compelled by him. He was doing everything I dreamed of, and he was having adventures, while I was sitting there and letting my life just waste away. I had a nothing job, a nothing relationship, just fantasies.

"He finally helped me start to live some of them out. I loved it—all of it. He introduced me to people who could take sex and make it something magical. I . . . I'd never known what to do with it; sex, I mean. Honestly. I just knew it was this huge force, and I knew I wasn't in charge of it; I knew I wasn't taking full advantage of it. But these people created worlds around it, they performed entire plays, they developed new characters. Every time I met a new one of them, I'd get swept up in it. I wanted more. I wanted as much of the magic as I could get.

"He told me about . . . this. He said I might want to consider it. He told me it was the furthest I could go. I could also get some money together, more than I could ever have made at home. And I'd know, finally, if this was what I wanted for my life."

He nodded. "I think I can understand."

"Was it the same for you?"

Andre looked at me suddenly. His face was blank for a moment; then he laughed. "Can anything like this ever be 'the same' for two people? I mean, all the elements are similar, but the stories that people have about getting here have to be so . . . different. We aren't talking about walking the same street to get to the train station in the morning, you know?" He laughed again. "But maybe, in its own way, it is the same.

"No. I don't think that's true. I came my own way." He looked away from me for a moment, scanning the rest of the room. There wasn't anything interesting going on, but I don't think he expected there to be. I think he just wanted to look away from me to get his mind in some kind of order.

"I grew up," he began, "in a suburb of Des Moines. I was the only black kid. My parents were professionals and the type of blacks that thought—that desperately wanted to believe—that the color of their skin didn't make any difference.

"Our town was small and polite, and everyone, in his own way, was withdrawn and quiet. It was an easy place for my parents to live out their fantasy. I never thought much about things. I just spent my time with my books and never had any trouble with the rest of the kids in school. I can look back now and realize it was easy for me. I never attempted those things that would have created trouble. I never dated white girls, I never even really knew I was thinking about men, so I never came on to the other boys.

"Then, in my junior year of high school, we got a new gym teacher. He was the biggest, blackest man I'd ever seen." Andre's smile changed when that memory came into focus in his mind. His face lit up, as though he were thinking of something very funny and extremely sensual, both at the same time. "He hated me on sight. I had never known anyone to have that kind of feeling about me. If they had it, they sure never showed it to me.

"I insulted the man just by being there. I couldn't understand it. There was no way I could please him. I was never good at athletics, but I wasn't bad at the things we had to do in gym class. He made the whole thing a living hell. He singled me out for criticism, and when he gave it, it was cruel, insulting, degrading.

"One day, I just out and out confronted him after class. 'Why are you giving me such a bad time?' I asked him. 'Because you're soft,' he said. 'A black boy's gotta be hard, harder than those whites.' I barely understood what he was talking about; we didn't even really have black magazines in my parents' house. It was Iowa. There just wasn't any reality about it to make me understand.

"I did understand, though, that it had a lot to do with this man and how he felt about himself. He was as dark-skinned as I'm light. I either have a lot of white blood in me or my ancestors are from Ethiopia or one of the other parts of Africa where they have thin lips and slender noses. This man's people must have been from the heart of the continent. He had thick lips, a flat nose, and flared nostrils.

"And, like it or not, his presence brought out some of that reality throughout the school year. I was the kind of black that white people can ignore. I was smart and quiet and had a pretty face. But he was a black buck, a stud with muscles and those African features. He was so well-defined that his legs—we could see them in class; he only wore gym shorts—were like big slabs of meat. His thighs were built of huge pieces of flesh that were hard and moved strongely under his skin.

"I was furious at him for coming into my world and messing it up that way. He not only gave me a hard time, but now I had to listen to words from my classmates that I'd never had to hear before. 'Nigger.' 'Jungle bunny.' All the rest of them. Even if they were using those words to describe him, they were talking about me at the same time. I knew that.

"I didn't know what to do with that anger. But I decided that at least I wouldn't take his shit. I started to work out at home, something I'd never done before. I was determined I'd at least stop him from making a fool of me in class.

"I got better, but it was a slow process; neither he nor I noticed it over that school year. But the next summer, I worked even harder. I'd convinced my parents to get me a set of weights, and I spent the whole vacation working with them.

"It was the most physical thing I'd ever done in my life, working with those weights. My parents had wanted me to forget I had dark skin. I'd gone further. I'd forgotten I had a body. Now I drove myself. I forced myself to go to the limits of my endurance every single day. All the time I was doing it, I had this picture of him in front of me. I could see his nappy hair and his huge muscles, and I remembered once when I'd seen him wearing a jock, nothing more, with his big, muscular black ass outlined by the white waistband and straps, right there where I could see every part of it.

"My workouts became erotic, so sexual I couldn't help the way my cock would get hard. I'd be looking in the mirror while I was lifting weights and see this thick dick pushing against my cock. I kept picturing him watching me while I did it, while I sweated and strained and cursed at him for making me do it. But I'd never stop. I just kept right on going with it. And I kept the image of that huge man in my mind. I built up my size and my strength, and I was ready for him when the school year began.

"I walked into his office before the first gym class that next year. I knew that my body was looking good. My T-shirt was stretched tight across my chest, and my old shorts were too small around the thighs now. I looked at him. He was staring at my chest, then at my crotch. He was worrying about something. I suddenly understood. All the strange, erotic thoughts I'd had that summer came back to me. They hadn't just happened. They'd been there because somehow I'd known that he wanted me.

"That's when I experienced a whole new emotion. Power. I knew that he'd been thinking about me all summer himself. I knew he was in my power. I knew I could make him do things. That's what my pretty face and my new body meant. I hated him all the more for that. He'd already come into my small little world and torn away the polite fictions that meant I never had to think of myself as a nigger. That was bad enough. Now, when he was looking at me and wanting me, he made me see I was a fag, too. Because the way he looked meant I had to take all those images I'd had and all those times my cock'd gotten hard and understand that it was because I was that way as much as he was.

"I leaned over his desk; I was furious. I looked him dead in the eye, and I said. 'If I can't do more of every exercise than anyone else in this class, nigger, you can fuck my ass.'

"He didn't say a word, but he didn't look scared. He just sat there. I went and lined up with the rest of the seniors. He finally came out with his shorts on and his whistle around his neck and all the rest of the stuff that gym teachers have, carrying his clipboard. He had us all go through a whole series of different exercises, like we had to do every fall to be able to set our goals for the year.

"I won every single event. I did more of everything than anyone else: push-ups, sit-ups, you name it. I would have, anyhow, but it was because of him that I did them all so easily. I had adrenaline flowing through my system like I'd never experienced before. I was in a fury. I wasn't satisfied to just do more than anyone else. I did them at the fastest pace possible. I raced through every part of it.

"But then we got to the last thing, the pull-ups. There was a big white jock in the class, one of the guys on the football team. I can't remember the exact number of pull-ups he'd done, but I went up for my turn, and I started to swing up and down from that bar like crazy. I was counting out loud, and then, at the very moment I got to the number the other guy'd done, I stopped. Everyone knew I could do more. I wasn't even winded; there hadn't been any strain. But I hung from the bar and stared at that teacher. Then I dropped down onto the floor and walked back to my place in line.

"It was amazing. I had the most amazing feelings I'd ever had in my life right then. He couldn't meet my eyes afterwards. We were both remembering what I'd said to him in his office, and that was the only thing that mattered. He had always been supercool, supercontrolled. But now he lost it. He could hardly get through the rest of the class.

"It was the last period of the morning. After this was lunch. They never took attendance in the cafeteria. I knew that. I waited for a few minutes for everyone else to run through his shower and get out. Then, when I was sure we were alone, I went into his office. It was just a cubicle off the locker room. He was there, and he looked up when I walked in but didn't say a word. He stood up, and it seemed like he was trying to get out the words to make me leave him alone.

"But I didn't give him a chance. I pulled off my shirt and threw it in a corner. Then I pulled down my shorts and my jock. I bent over his desk. 'Come on, nigger, fuck my ass. I made a deal. I'm keeping it.'

"He didn't move at first; he just stood there. When he did walk behind me, his motions were mechanical, as though they were being done against his will. Then, for the first time in my life, I felt another man's hand on my butt. He ran the edge of his palm up and down my crack. He couldn't help himself. He wanted it too badly.

"He got something out of his other pants' pocket, out of his wallet. I heard him pull down his own shorts then, and I figured he was putting on a rubber. In a minute, there was the blunt end of his cock pressing against my hole. He wet it with something. Then it went in. He fucked me hard, in just a couple strokes. It was over before it began. That was all it took, he was so hot for me.

"I stood up afterwards and just willed myself not to let him know how much it had hurt. No one had ever fucked me. I didn't want him to know that, either. I didn't want him to know how important it'd been. I wanted to keep all my power. I wanted that badly.

"He started to act guilty. That proved to me that I had won. I just smiled at him and left and went to take a shower.

"The rest of the school year, he fucked me at least twice a week, or else I sucked him, or something sexual happened. He never wanted to do it, he said. But he couldn't resist me when I came on to him.

"It was amazing, because I'd never really experienced any emotion before. Never. I don't know how to explain that. But my world had been so quiet, so protected, and now I was in the middle of this thing with him, and it was full of stuff so potent that I'd get dizzy when it all came over me at once.

"I loved him. I hated him. He'd come into my world and made me really look at a black man with kinky hair and dark skin, and he made me know that's what the world really thought of me. Worse, he looked at my body, and he wanted it, and when I knew that, I had to admit that I wanted him, too. He came into my world and took away the lies. It was wonderful when it happened. It was terrible, too. And it was all his fault that when I woke up in the morning and looked in the mirror, I knew I was a nigger fag. I could have lied forever if it hadn't been for him. But now I couldn't.

"The worst part—the very worst part—was that he fell in love with me. By the end of the first semester, he was already that way. He wanted everything to be nice then. He wanted me to come to his apartment, where he'd make me drinks or give me back rubs or be able to figure excuses so I could spend the night with him in his bed. I didn't want any of that. I wanted everyone in the whole world to be honest to the two of us and have a reason to call us what they thought we were: nigger fags. I didn't want any more lies. And most of all, I didn't want to have those powerful emotions weakened in any way. The spirits had been let loose. I didn't want them pushed back into a new façade of respectability. I wanted them to dance.

"I went away to college, and though he wrote to me, I never answered; I never talked to him again. He wanted to let those emotions of mine dilute into a soft kind of liking and an even softer kind of lovemaking. I still wanted to hate and love at the same time and to feel power and rage. Once I'd tasted all of that, the softness was nothing. It was sleeping. I wanted to be awake again.

"I was ready for college, at least as far as sex was concerned. I'm good-looking; I know it. Anyone that was ever going to think about fucking a black man was going to want my ass. I had them lined up. But I'd throw them away just as quickly. They all wanted that same easy stuff the gym instructor had wanted. They wanted to come into my room late at night and make love and read poetry and all of that.

"I was still looking for a gym instructor who'd fuck me over his desk.

"I used to do dangerous things—the worst things you could imagine—just to sense those feelings in another man. I used to try and find the most red necked football-player types who'd been recruited from the South, the ones who'd never have gotten past the front gates if they hadn't been star athletes.

"I used to love the ones who'd give in, who'd go to bed with me because they wanted a piece of a man's ass but didn't dare look for it themselves. I'd come and gotten them; they didn't think they had any options. They'd be fucking me, and I could see the hatred they had for me, not just because I was black but because I'd known they wanted me.

"A couple of them, when they were just ready to come, would even dare say it to me. 'Feel my cock up your ass, nigger fag.' When they did, I knew they looked at me and they had these feeble minds that were thinking back to the old days when they could have just gone to some auction in Charleston or New Orleans and they could have bought someone like me. They were furious that they couldn't anymore.

"But it was all right, because, you see, I had them. Because they would fall just as hard as the rest of them. There was one—a real hard-ass from Alabama—who'd even started bringing me flowers. He had it so bad for me, he was willing to risk doing that in front of the whole dorm.

"I learned these men were captured. They were easy prey. I could make them do anything I chose. I'd make them beg to be able to fuck me. But it wasn't any good because when they gave in, then the emotions—that love and hatred and disgust and euphoria—were all gone, and I just felt something weak for them, mainly pity.

"I got to go to Chicago every once in a while. I walked into a leather bar there once, and I knew I was closer to what I wanted than I'd ever been before. I stood there and saw all these men with their uniforms and their leather and their hard looks and figured that maybe I could feel those emotions with them. I started to make up all the excuses I could to get to Chicago after that, and every night I was in the city I went to that bar.

"They were exciting, and they were able to produce feelings in me that made me come alive. They brought back the fear and the rest of it, and I felt it all over again. I loved them—God, I used to love them—because they made me experience those things so powerfully.

"The first time I was tied up and couldn't move, couldn't escape from my captor, just nearly flipped me out totally. And the first time a man used a whip on me. And the first time one made me eat out of a dog dish on my hands and knees. Each one of those things would just wind me up, send me out there into a new place. I loved every single man who'd do it; no matter how horrible it was, I got those emotions.

"But they'd fuck it up; each and every one of them would. Because he'd show me some other side of himself. The man with the whip wanted to take me to the opera. The man with the bondage was a college professor in the same field as my major and wanted to tutor me. The guy with the dog dish wanted me to switch roles and force him to do the same thing.

"I wanted to know that what I was feeling was real. I didn't want to playact those things. They were too beautiful to be changed so carelessly.

"You see, I always remembered what the option was: the life I'd led in my parents' house, where eyes were blind and flesh didn't feel and the real world didn't exist. If I gave up this quest—this desire to be on the edge, the outer limit—I knew I'd go back to that, and I knew that was a life of living death.

"There was one man in that bar in Chicago who I never did make it with. But I knew he always was checking me out. I also learned quickly enough that they all spoke to one another, that they passed around information on new faces the way they might discuss the availability of theater tickets. The others would have told him about me.

"One night, he came up to me and said he wanted to talk to me. We went to another bar nearby, one that was less crowded, more comfortable for a private conversation. We sat there, and he began to describe this secret world where things weren't fake, where they didn't play games and where the masters' powers were absolute. He offered to take me into that world if I wanted. I got a rush as powerful as the first time with that gym teacher because this was much more; it went much further. This was going over the edge."

Andre looked at me. He shrugged. He smiled again. "I'm here. I'm on my great adventure. I have three years to find out what I can do with reality. I can only begin to imagine how much I'm going to hate whoever buys me and how much I'm going to hate everything he does to me—or she does to me. But I'm going to love that person too. I just know I'm going to spend three years feeling strong things about someone, and I'm going to have to know that the person owns me, at least all of my body. Then I'll know. I'll know if it was just something that needed to be done or if it's something I want forever. Because it could be just something that I had to have to make up for all the years I never felt anything at all—just could be . . ."

3

Peter

The six of us jumped to our feet as soon as we heard the door. Peter and the other servant came in and began speaking at once: "Come on, in a line, starting over here." They made us move quickly, using our shoulders to guide us until we were in the formation they wanted.

Peter stood in front of us, his hands back on his waist. "The first thing you can do is stop trying to cover yourselves." There was another sneer on his face as he mocked us for having put our hands over our groins. "You'll have to learn to love being naked. They always remind you of that. Even when you are given clothes"—he picked at his shirt—"they usually do something like this—give you silk clothes that cling to your body and remind you of it all the more.

"There's no escaping nakedness in this life. You have to learn to accept that.

"Now"—he began to walk up and down the line—"here's what will be happening to you tonight. We're going to prepare you for the sale. You all have to be douched, your hair cut, your nails manicured. The whole idea is that you must be as good-looking as you can be.

"There'll be people coming in who are best at each one of these things. Stephen"—he nodded to the other servant—"and I are here to oversee their jobs—and you.

"When you're ready, we're going to take you to the sale room. There's no way I can explain what will really happen to you." He stopped walking and seemed to remember some faraway place. I thought that he was visualizing some other time rather than simply a location. His face appeared transformed for that one moment; all the bravado he'd shown while he had been ordering us about had disappeared.

It took a minute before he began again. "I can only promise you two things: You will cry, and you will be excited. There will be tears running down your cheeks, and your cocks will be hard or your cunts will be wet. There's no reason to fight either thing.

"They love them both—the tears and the sexual turn-on. And that's the major lesson you have to learn: Everything is for them from now on."

He moved over toward me and grabbed hold of my biceps. He didn't speak as he led me to the shower area. There was a long metal hose attached to one of the outlets. He picked it up with his other hand. "Bend over." I stared at him, unable to move. The command was too blunt, the demand too severe. I looked around wildly and tried to wrench my arm away from his grip.

He only laughed at me. "They're not going to help you," he said. "They've all made the same agreement you have. Now, stop being so stupid and bend over; let me see that pretty, hairy ass of yours close up.

"And get used to it; this is just child's play compared to what's going to be happening to you later on."

Andre was staring at me from across the room. His face was frozen, his arms were crossed over his chest as though he were cold, but the room's temperature only seemed to be climbing. Somehow I got my body to lean forward.

Someone giggled just as the nozzle forced itself past my muscles and inside me. There was a sudden tremendous pressure in me as the water began to flow. I closed my eyes in dread over this demonstration—the one they were providing the others and the one that I was putting on myself by not resisting in any way.

I had to think of something else—anything but that cold metal that was spewing water inside me. I forced my eyes open and looked over to Andre. His cock was getting hard as he stood there studying me and what I was going through. The thick length was lifting up, away from his thighs. I turned away from him. I wasn't sure if he was being turned on by my humiliation or by his own fantasy of being in my place.

I forced myself to think of the strong arms that were holding on to me. I forgot what they were doing and willed my mind to just focus on their touch. One of Peter's arms reached over me and thèn down around my belly. I was resting on it as though it were a sling. His big hand was gripping my side. I could feel the hard sinews of his forearm as it pressed against my softer stomach. His skin was bare where we touched, and the feel of it was warm and intimate. I realized he must've had this done to him, maybe often. I struggled with that idea, wanting to cling to it because it meant I wasn't alone. We were together.

Somehow I stopped thinking of him as someone who was doing something bad to me—something painful and degrading. Instead, I thought of him as someone who was in my same position. It made it easier to just be there and let him shove the nozzle in and out and to calmly follow his instructions: Hold in the water; let it out; spread my legs more; tighten my ass.

I kept staring straight ahead. I didn't want to watch the actual evidence, the stuff that was being flushed out of my body. The sound of it all and of the water running from the faucets was already too real; there was too much gone. I was only there to be controlled, to follow instructions.

He stood me up suddenly after I'd followed his orders to

force out the accumulated water after the third flushing. He was smiling at me. "Come on, over here. We have to do it once more with something that will make you smell good. We don't want their precious selves to have to take the chance of catching a whiff of reality."

He took me over to another corner of the tiled area. He sat down and slapped his knee, an obvious signal that he wanted me to bend over it. I got down on my knees and leaned over. I was still trying to focus on him. I was able to do it more easily now. I could feel the fleshy mound of his genitals when my belly was lowered onto them.

He spanked my ass playfully. "Spread them apart and make this easy on both of us," he said. I hurried to comply. I wondered for a moment if my fantasy of who he was and what he was doing was actually taking over my mind, because it felt as though he suddenly became very gentle as he inserted a small rubber bulb's head up my already sore anus. But even when it'd been done, his palm stayed on my ass and seemed to move around it with something that certainly felt like a caress.

"Enough!" He slapped me again and guided me to my feet when he was done. I was light-headed from the enemas, feeling as though my energy had been flushed out with everything else. He either expected that or else I might have looked pale, because he assured me the sensation was only natural and that it'd pass.

"That last stuff is made from herbs." he explained. "Hold it for a while; then let it go on the toilet. Make sure you get rid of all of it. It'll leave you smelling good, not perfumed, really, just clean. They'll like that." He seemed to be suddenly a little sad. He put a hand on my side and squeezed me slightly. "Go on, back to the line. There'll be more people here for you in a minute or two. I have work to do."

The next person Peter took care of was Gene, the man who'd been standing alone. He wasn't ready for the procedure and began to physically fight against Peter. The whole room went stock-still with tension when he reached up and hit Peter in the face.

Was this authentic? Suddenly the question was horribly real. Would someone get away with behavior like that? Was there some magic force that was going to come down from the ceiling and remove Gene's dissident presence from us? What really happens to a slave who rebels in this world?

"Stupid idiot," Peter said quietly. He rubbed a hand on his chin where Gene's blow had landed. Two other servants came into the room. They started to move toward Gene. "No," Peter said. "That would be too easy."

He walked up to the naked man, Gene, and touched him on the shoulder. "You'd actually like that, wouldn't you? If I let them beat you? They'd do it, you know. But I'm not going to have them touch you. It would let you off the hook.

"If they *forced* you to take this hose up your ass, it wouldn't be the same. It'd start ruining everything. Then you could forget that you signed the contract. You could make believe you were a victim, that this wasn't your decision. But it was; you're the one who chose to come here.

"When you did, you gave up everything. Everything." Peter whispered the word in a way that gave it an eerie emphasis. "You're the only person who could have sold yourself into slavery. You have to understand that every day for the rest of your contract. If you don't, you'll fail. I'm not sure why you did it and why these others did. Sometimes I'm not even sure why I signed my own contract. But after looking at every possible reason, I know that you'll lose it all if it becomes a matter of brute force.

"It's an easy out, something that you can hold inside yourself, maybe, and justify many things. But it doesn't work.

"Now, what you're going to do is this: You're going to get down on your hands and knees, and you're going to crawl over to the hose. You're going to pick it up with your teeth, and you're going to bring it back to me. You're going to do it because you're going to prove to yourself that you're sure you wanted to sign that contract Mr. Cantrell gave you. You're going to do it because you know you'll be crawling for however many years you said you'd sell yourself.

"Get on your knees. Crawl."

We watched as Gene slowly collapsed onto the floor. The rebellion had been erased from his face. There was nothing but defeat on it now, defeat and shame. He moved slowly at first; his motion toward the hose was tentative in the beginning.

Then something about him changed. The stress of moving on his hands and knees brought out lines in Gene's torso that I hadn't seen when he was standing upright. There were muscles that were more sharply etched because of his position and his movement. He looked more handsome, stronger. His flanks appeared especially sleek, and the flesh there moved in a way that made me think of velvet as his skin kept a tight hold on the undulating body.

He did it; Gene followed the order. He brought the hose back in his mouth. Peter took it and used a hand to signal to Gene that he shouldn't get up. Still on his hands and knees, Gene submitted to the intrusion of the steel tube into his anus. When Peter ordered him to spread his legs even further, he did. And after the humiliation of having us all watch, his cleaning was done. Gene moved over to one of the shelves, where he sat, curled up, with his arms clinging to his legs, and softly cried.

As I watched the display, my thoughts altered, just as Gene's appearance had changed when he'd gotten on his hands and knees and moved across the floor. I knew that all of the rest of the slaves-about-to-be were going through the same transformation I was. We were no longer thinking about being chosen or about how attractive we were. We were finally realizing how real this all was. We were frightened, scared to the depths of our bellies. You could smell it on us. The warm room with the constant running showers began to stink with the fear-induced sweat that cascaded from our skin.

The rest of Cantrell's servants began to work on us. One of them trimmed my hair. I'd been ordered not to have it cut for at least a couple weeks before the auction—a master might want to have me in longer hair than usual, I was told. This servant only took off the most obvious straggles. Then he put me on one of the benches and went about shaving me.

He used a straight-edged razor to scrape my face. The terror of that piece of sharp steel in someone else's hands tore me apart more than anything else. But the worst of it was the erection it gave me as well. It seemed, in that weird moment, that every swipe of the blade was an act of lovemaking, and I was sure that I was going to come at one point.

When the man said, "Spread your legs," I thought he was just teasing me or was going to tease me about the hard cock that was rising up off my belly. But I wasn't going to argue with him. As soon as I'd complied, he smeared shaving cream over my testicles. I looked at them and then at him in disbelief. Surely they weren't going to . . .

"Just your balls," he said, as though he could read my mind. "That's all." He grabbed hold of my testicles and pulled them down sharply. Then the razor that had seemed so erotic when he was using it on my face began to work in broad strokes up and down my sac. He rolled my balls in his palm as he went, using areas he'd already shaved to hold on to while he completed the next stage of his job.

I nearly lost it then. It wasn't the dull pain from his squeezing my balls. I'd known he could cut me when he'd shaved my face. Being close to danger in that way—a way that seemed more symbolic than real—had turned me on. But having that danger focused on my sex this way was too much. It meant too much. My heart seemed to beat impossibly fast; my senses got confused. But my erection stayed hard.

"There." He stood up and used a towel to wipe the last of the shaving cream off. "Now, just sit and wait. When they're all done, you'll take a final shower, and we'll powder your body a bit to fight the odor and the sweat. Then you'll be ready."

He patted my shoulder and walked away. I stared down at the red surface of my balls. I hadn't seen that part of my body look that way in years. It had been covered with a thick coating of hair ever since I was a boy. But now it was gone, just one more thing I had lost by signing up for this. I looked farther up at the thick coat on my chest and suddenly realized that after tonight someone could decide that it should go as well.

What would I be left with? What would still be mine? I shuddered a little bit and wasn't sure I knew the answer—or if there was an answer that mattered.

I sat silently and waited while the rest of them were finished. No one put up the least resistance; certainly not Gene. They all went through the same shaving as I did. The women's pubic hair wasn't all removed. Just as we men didn't have to lose all of ours, only that on our testicles, the women's was only shaped to make sure their triangular bush was nicely symmetrical.

When everyone had been taken care of, we were sent back under the showers. When I was done, Peter was waiting for me, holding a huge bath towel. He wrapped it around my shoulders and guided me to a far corner of the room, where he began to briskly wipe me dry.

"You look good," he said in a low voice as his hands worked on my back. They were rough as they toweled me, moving farther down. He reached my ass, and I could feel the towel going up and down my crack, purposely paying a lot of attention to my hole. Then he turned me around. He smiled when he saw that his attention had stiffened my cock back up again.

He spread his hands under the towel and placed them both against my chest so that a fabric-covered palm was directly over each of my nipples. Then he rubbed even harder than before. "Yeah, very good-looking." He smiled. He kept it up for a long time, confusing me. I didn't know how to respond.

He moved back and pulled his T-shirt off and tossed it onto the shelf beside us. His skin was smooth; the only strands of hair were those that came from out of his underarms. He moved back toward me with the towel. His chest was extraordinary, and his nipples were pronounced. They both seemed as erect as my cock.

"Suck them," he whispered as the towel wrapped around my chest and his hands drew me toward him. I felt so powerless in this place. I'd signed the paper. But I hadn't been bought. Did that mean everyone was my master, even another slave? I wanted to find some way to deny that possibility; there was some small part of me that couldn't let it be true. But more of me was swept away by the idea that my body was there for whoever wanted to use it, no matter what the use. I followed his instruction and brought one of the well-developed nipples into my mouth. He sighed as soon as my tongue began to move the hard flesh back and forth.

"Feel my cock," he whispered in my ear. "Take it in your hand." I reached down against the silk shorts and found a thick tube of flesh beneath the cloth. I grabbed hold of it. I was the one who sighed now. I have never gotten over the sensation of the touch of a heavy, blood-filled cock. Never.

"Peter!" A voice spoke urgently beside us. It was Stephen. "Stop it! Cantrell would take the skin off your back if he knew you were doing this to one of them."

Peter roughly pushed me away and began toweling me again. "Damn you . . ."

"Don't damn me," Stephen answered. "You were being a

fool. It's absolutely against the rules for you to play with these people. You know that. And you know what he's been saying about your attitude recently."

"I have every right . . ."

"You have no right," Stephen said. "Don't you remember what you just said to that other guy? Whatever else, Peter, remember that you're the one who's signed on for a third contract. You can't say you didn't know what you were getting into. You knew better than almost anyone else what was going on when you put your name on that paper.

"Jesus, man, what's getting into you, anyway? You volunteer for another three years and then start pulling this shit? There are lots more interesting ways to have your masochism relieved than the kinds of things you're pulling on him."

"Don't you ever want to know what it's like?" Peter finally said. "Don't you want to know what it's like to be one of them? One of the masters?

"I've spent all these years like this, in The Network, and I've never understood what it would be like to be one of them. The games Cantrell has us play with one another don't count. It's not the same thing at all. But I see someone like this"—he played with some of the hairs on my chest—"and I wonder what I could do with him if I had him for all those years.

"Don't you think they get bored? Or do they really love us so much? Or do they hate us?"

"Peter, this isn't going to help . . ." But Stephen wasn't able to really say anything. He seemed disturbed by the idea, and I understood somehow that it was because he did wonder, just the way Peter did.

The blond slave let go of my body. He put a hand on my arm, squeezing it almost painfully. "I'll have so much money when this contract is over, Stephen, that I could go to the first auction afterwards and spend it and then own someone like this. What would I do? What would you do?"

"I'd stop wasting time and risking finding out just what the hell Cantrell would do to me if he walked in right now. Peter, he could take the skin off your back for something like this, and you know it. Come on. Leave it alone. Don't make things so difficult. There'll be more than enough fun tonight, during the sale. Just get back to work."

Stephen walked away, and Peter went back to finishing his job of drying me off. He spent much too long on my hard cock and on massaging my thighs. I watched his hands move over my body, and I kept on trying to catch his eyes. I wanted to see inside them and try to figure out some of the things he'd been saying. Because even if he was a slave right now, he'd had those thoughts, and I was anxious to find out what a master did think of his slave. My cock got hard as he kept on feeling me; this man could be a master, and just being this close to him was turning me on.

He had me wait on the side while the rest of them were finished up. We were lined up again, our skin bright from all the cleaning and the rubbing. Our faces were starting to fill with anticipation. The event was getting closer. The excitement was beginning to overcome the fear.

"You're going to be put on the blocks now," Stephen announced. "You'll be chained with gold links at your ankles and your knees to the glass surface. That's the traditional means of displaying a slave at one of The Network's auctions. It lets the buyer see you from every angle before he or she makes a choice. You're going to have to kneel all the time—believe me, the sale is no time for any displays of independence or revolt.

"Your wrists are going to be chained to a gold collar that will be placed around your neck. You'll be on view for at least two hours before the auction actually begins. You will do everything they tell you to do—*everything*. Peter's already told you what you can minimally expect.

"You will cry, and you will get turned on. Your cocks and

cunts are going to drip because you're so hot after a while. There's no way you can hide that part of it. And your tears will be just as real and just as obvious. Everyone expects both.

"You are never to speak unless they ask you a direct question. Ever. If you do, you'll be severely punished. They probably won't speak to you, by the way. Don't worry about planning any speeches. For your own sakes, realize you are a slave.

"You've had fantasies before; I know it. And you've all probably played out a lot of them. But this is different; this is much, much different. This has reality weaved into it, and one part of that reality is the punishment these people can bring down on you. Pay attention to those small rules and you can make it through the night."

And the rest of it? Just pay attention to a few small rules and could I make it through the next three years as well?

4

The Auction

My knees were already sore from the hard glass surface. The gold chains around my neck, wrists, and ankles and at my knees were just as cold. The breeze in the big room was a relief from the intense heat of the other room, if that was any consolation at all. I was desperately trying to find that consolation in anything.

I kept turning around to look toward the door that was behind me. They were back there. I could hear the laughing and the jingle of glasses. They were drinking their champagne without a care in the world. They were enjoying themselves. While on the other side of that mahogany door—on this side—there were six people waiting to be sold.

I turned back around and saw Andre looking at me. He was smiling more broadly than I'd seen him so far. "How can you look so happy?" I asked.

"It's over," he answered. "There's nothing left but accepting it all." He took a deep breath and rested back on his haunches.

I looked down beyond him, to the far end of the row, and saw that one of the women was fulfilling Peter's prophecy. She was already in tears, and her high, pointed breasts were rising and falling with sobs that I could hear clearly.

Directly on my other side was the couple. They were whispering to one another, though I couldn't hear their words and had no idea which was comforting the other. They were sharing a single cube, another indication that they were to be sold as a pair and not separately, like the rest of us. They could lean toward the center, stretching against their gold chains, and kiss occasionally, as though that small gesture could get them through this ordeal.

Ordeal. That was the word that best described all of this. It was infinitely worse than any of the rest of it. I could look down and see the underside of my balls and my anus reflecting back up off the glass. My arms were secured behind my neck, and my legs were firmly attached to the cube. There was no position I could possibly assume that would allow me even the slightest self-defense.

The way I was being displayed forced me to be aware of my complete vulnerability. There was that slight breeze that would move against my tits and make the nipples more sensitive than they already were. My balls were hanging down and couldn't even touch the sides of my thighs. My ass cheeks were spread apart, and I could feel the clean, tiny hole as the wind played with it.

But all the awareness was nothing compared to the thought of those people who were behind that closed door. They would soon come walking through, carrying their wineglasses and walking around us—browsing, deciding which of us was worth their time and money.

Peter and Stephen were working at last-minute details, moving among the chairs and couches that were facing our tables and straightening decorations and arranging pieces of furniture. They would occasionally look at us, smiling or running over to correct some minute detail about how we were being shown off.

Stephen was more indulgent of Peter now that they were the only other ones with us. When Peter would come over and stroke my cock, teasing it up into an erection, Stephen's reprimands weren't as vehement as they had been in the other room.

The reason became obvious when Stephen began to pay increasing attention to the crying woman at the end of the line. He had no interest in calming her down, at least none that I could see. He seemed to enjoy her discomfort and her tears and added to both by moving to her side and leaning over her. This wasn't a transgression of the rules evidently, not in the sense that Peter had violated them with me. This was only a part of the household's duties—getting the slaves in the proper frame of mind for the auction.

I watched the first time as Stephen's finger disappeared up her vagina. He muffled her loud cries with a kiss and wouldn't relieve the pressure until he got her to thrust her hips backward and forward in response to his invasions.

I wasn't the only one who was receiving Peter's attentions. Andre was just as interesting to him. Peter stood between us and stroked both of our asses. His touch was much more gentle than Stephen's was, or appeared to be. But the effect was the same, and so was his insistence on our responding to him. He wouldn't leave us until both Andre and I were sitting straight up in our kneeling position, our cocks growing harder as his fingers lightly stroked our assholes. Then, smirking with pleasure, he'd walk away and leave us alone with those stiff cocks and the fantasies that his touch had created.

Finally, the doors opened.

I felt my muscles tighten, and I had to will myself not to turn to watch them enter. I didn't want to give them that pleasure so easily—that knowledge that I was as anxious as I honestly was. I knelt back on the glass, feeling the pain of the hard surface against my legs, and stared straight ahead.

Who were they? Who were these strangers who would risk so much by being at a place like this? I remembered all the thoughts I'd had before about the risks being taken by people who'd dare flaunt society so much that they would attend a sale of living human beings. I made up scandalized newspaper headlines in my mind. I imagined careers being ruined and families being torn apart by the truth about these people.

But as I always did, I also knew I loved them for that very reason. I felt the fear drain away—at least a little bit of it—and I pictured the fraternity that bound us together, the people who went into this thing for the sheer pleasure of it, to experience the utter decadence and revel in the extremes we were all exploring.

Somehow those thoughts gave me back some small piece of pride—that I had made a decision and a choice. I looked down at my body and remembered how hard I'd worked to prepare it for this sale. There'd been hours of working out, and there'd been just as much time receiving the lessons from the man who'd helped me ready myself for this moment.

The voices behind me were getting louder, and there seemed to be more of them. In a moment, just a single moment, there would be people in front of me who would inspect me. I lifted up a bit higher on my knees, wanting to be ready for them. . . .

"A male? Why would you want a male, Alice?"

One of the two women who were standing in front of me was clamping the sharp edges of two of her fingernails hard against one another, trapping one of my nipples between them.

"He's quite attractive." That was all my torturer said.

"But I wouldn't think you'd like all this hair." The other woman raked her own long nails across my chest.

"It could be shaved off." The woman called Alice twisted my tit harder in the other direction and sent a new shock wave of pain through my body. "He'd look quite adorable then, in an androgynous fashion."

"No, darling, come on and leave him alone. You're simply

playing with him. There's the lovely girl down on the end, much more something we might be interested in."

My nipple was released quickly, and I collapsed back on my haunches now that the agony was over. Peter had been right on both accounts: I was in tears. And my cock was hard.

I was furious with it! It was pointing straight up in the air, and the slit at the top of my glans was wet from the continuing ooze of seminal fluid that leaked from it. I hadn't wanted those two women—as beautiful as they were in their extravagant evening clothes—to see that. But they had. Those same long, sharp nails had enjoyed scratching at the edges of my glans, sending wonderful shivers through every part of my body—and my mind.

Each of the people who stopped and looked at me could be my destiny for the next three years. There was no way to escape that. I remembered the words of Mr. Cantrell—that The Network was relentless in tracking down those of us who might ever dare break a contract—and I believed him. I believed every word he said.

I got my breathing and tears under control just as the next buyer approached. A hand came out and only had to touch my nipples to get a shudder in response. They'd been handled so roughly by so many people that any contact was excruciating.

"Yes," the man said softly, "very nice." I looked up at him. He was the most frightening one yet. He appeared to be about fifty. He was dressed in a business suit and carried both a cigar and a champagne glass in one hand. He reached down and picked up the leather folio that sat on the edge of my table. He put down the champagne glass to hold the folder more easily. He read through it, occasionally looking up at me and smiling.

I knew that my contract was there. On it were the limitations of my servitude—which were almost nonexistent. I could not be permanently damaged, of course. Nor could I be tattooed or marked by other means. I couldn't have my citizenship put in jeopardy; if I were taken out of the country, it had to be done legally and with my real passport. The term of service was three years from this very date. I was to be paid handsomely, but those were the only restrictions.

"He could stud for Zoli," the man said to the other male, who stood behind him. "He would father a very handsome child."

I felt as if a fist had exploded into my stomach. I was ready to scream out. That was the one thing I'd never thought of. I'd known that I could be bought by women; it was a possibility from which I'd been told I couldn't exempt myself. But actually having children? They couldn't do that—they wouldn't; would they ever do anything that extreme? This was supposed to be an erotic slavery; that was the real limit. I tried to convince myself that the two men were simply toying with me, terrorizing me and hoping that I'd entertain them with my panic.

"No, Donald. I don't see it. She would never agree, and that is a restriction in her contract, you know. You haven't any real use for a male in your household; it's much more up my alley."

My mind still refused to register their threat as being real. I had to insist to myself that it was only a kind of psychological warfare to make that kind of remark. It'd been difficult enough to get through the more concrete possibility that two women would have bought me. The images I conjured up of being the sexual servant to a female couple had sent me into enough of a panic. I couldn't go beyond that point.

The second man now reached down and cupped my balls. I'd learned quickly to accommodate those explorations. The one time I'd tried to draw back from such an intimate touch, the customer had only snapped his fingers and Peter had come running with a hard leather paddle that was used to emphasize just how much was expected of me.

"Very nice," the man said as I lifted up my midsection and moved it forward for him. He fondled me for a short while. "I haven't the need for a new one, unfortunately, and to load up my household would be a foolish use of money. I don't have it to waste the way people like Montclair do."

"I don't know if I'd call Montclair's lifestyle a waste—far from it. You're only jealous you can't afford it." The one called Donald seemed to still study me. "I haven't had a male slave in a long time; it could be great fun."

"If you're going to think of that kind of indulgence, you should consider them," the other said, pointing to the couple at the next table. "That could be interesting."

Donald smiled and put my folio back down on the table. "Yes, I think you're right."

The two men moved over to the waiting couple. I watched as Donald stood behind them and, reaching down, inserted a finger into the male's anus and one from the other hand in the woman's vagina. There was a much deeper smile on his face now.

A hand grabbed hold of my chin and wrenched it forward. He was a tall, dark-skinned black man, certainly the tallest person who'd walked past me so far. His tightly curled hair was close-cropped, and his face was clean-shaven. He was incredibly handsome. Even in his well-tailored suit I could sense the strength of his body.

He moved my head from side to side as though he wanted to study it from every angle. He let go of my chin after a bit, and his hand explored farther down. He moved from one nipple to the other, testing just how sensitive they'd become and evidently pleased by the quick responses he got. Then he took hold of my cock and stroked it roughly in his palm until it was totally erect.

He pressed a thumb against the head of it, pushing it against his palm. Then my balls were weighed, and he slapped them from side to side. Even though the pain was excruciating, there was something that was almost gentle about how he did it. He wasn't purposely trying to torture me, only to gauge the way I would react.

The hand was huge, and my balls felt insignificant in its grip. The fingers moved behind my balls, and one of them found the open and defenseless sphincter. It pushed a little at it and slipped in easily—the hole had been greased as part of our preparation.

I knew him. I looked at his face, and I recognized him as an athletic star I'd seen in ads or on television. He seemed to read my mind and smiled at me. There had been other fingers up my ass by now—men's and women's. But none of them had taken me so completely, nor had they stayed so long. He was moving his back and forth, making the pleasure agonizing.

I followed his gaze downward, and we could both see the new drop of fluid that seeped out of my cock and sat there on the tip in a perfect circle. He removed his finger—finally. It was as though that drop of fluid were some confession he'd demanded from me and he was satisfied once it'd been offered up to him. Stephen immediately appeared beside him with a tray that had a bowl of soapy water and a towel for him to clean with.

The black man went through the motions of washing, but all the time he was staring right at me. When his hands were dried and Stephen went on his way, the athlete picked up my folio and read from it. He nodded his head once or twice as he read, then returned it to the table.

He studied me some more, moving to the back of me and running a hand over my shoulders. Then he snapped his fingers. I knew what this meant as well. There was the sound of one of Cantrell's slave's bare feet on the floor behind me. I knew what was being delivered. Then the man finally spoke to me. "Bend down."

I took a breath and leaned forward until my forehead touched the surface of the table. My legs were spread so obscenely open that I could look back underneath and behind them and see the man's body as he positioned himself. Just before he swung, I saw the riding crop in his hand.

The pain was sharp and intense. I bit my lip to keep from yelling out. The crop slammed again onto my ass. They had done this to some of the others—tested them with crops and paddles to see how they could take a beating—but this was my first.

"Move your ass around," he said. His tone was infuriatingly casual. It was as if he weren't even giving orders or making demands, only making conversation. The crop hit again before I could figure out just what he wanted. "I said move it around!" Now there was a sense of authority in the way he spoke.

I rotated my hips, making myself feel more lewd than I ever had before in my life. "Better." But better wasn't something that he intended to reward me for. The crop landed again and again, finding its target no matter how fast I moved.

Suddenly, he stopped. The huge palm moved over first one cheek and then the other, as though he wanted to make sure my flesh had been heated up by his beating.

His hands went to my shoulders, urging me back up onto my knees. He moved around front with the crop still in his hands. He put it between my lips, and I fulfilled the obvious order to hold it in my mouth. Then he picked up the folio and took a pen out of his pocket. He wrote inside the folder. "I'm the first one to say he'll bid for you," the man said, his smile growing. "Spend some time thinking about living in Atlanta—spend some time thinking about living there three years." He took the crop out of my mouth and laid it on the mirrored table. He stared deeply once more.

Then he walked away.

I'd seen other people write in the folios, but I hadn't known why. But his statement made all the sense in the world; of course, that was it. They were indicating their interest in whichever of us they thought they might want to buy. This had been the only one who'd had that much interest in me. This one man, this one individual, could be the person who owned me.

The images raced through my mind—of my mouth running over his body and his huge muscles enclosed around me. I pictured his enormous physical power and the demands someone with his public schedule would make. There was fear and a sense of inadequacy as I tried to fantasize meeting all his requirements.

Then something totally different entered my mind. Something that struck me just as hard: He was the only one who'd been interested enough to write in that folder! Andre had had at least three men do that. But I was faced with the prospect of being humiliated by having only a single person who'd want me enough to pay for me.

I was overwhelmed by that idea—and embarrassed that I'd let it happen. I'd only cried when those two women had been working on my tits. I'd only been ashamed when another man had explored my ass. I hadn't given them anything else to make them want me. This was my own fault and my own doing.

I was determined not to be so involved in what was happening to the rest of them on their tables. I was lucky that even the last buyer had been so interested. After all, I hadn't even been waiting for someone to come up to me. I'd been looking in the opposite direction. That wouldn't happen again.

The next one to approach was dressed in a tuxedo. He was

blond and blue-eyed; his mustache was bleached almost white. He was nearly as tall as the last man but much leaner. He smiled at me, and I nodded back to him, hoping that my tears hadn't swollen my face too badly. This was going to be my chance to do everything much better.

He put down his glass and reached for my tits with both hands at once. I fought off the immediate impulse to move away and instead leaned forward to let my nipples meet his searching hands. I couldn't help but respond to the painful assault as he twisted and turned them both very harshly, but I refused to let my body retreat and kept my upper torso within his easy reach.

He released them, and a hand went to my balls. Again, I lifted myself up even more and gave him the access he wanted. "Very good," he said as he squeezed them much harder than anyone else had. I kept them there in the palm of his hand even when I might have moved backward.

He snapped his finger, and I heard the command once more: "Bend over." This time I not only complied but tried to do it gracefully, moving my body slowly in a single motion. I could look back through my legs as I had before. and I saw his tuxedo-clad thighs as he positioned himself and his crop.

The blows came faster and were even harder. But I didn't have to be told to move my ass for this master. I did it at once, even moving backward, as though I wanted to be closer to the crop as it delivered its stinging blows.

When it was over, he moved to the front of me. But he hadn't given me a command to kneel up, and I didn't dare do it on my own. That was lucky, because he obviously wanted me just the way I was.

He opened the folio and put it on my shoulders. Even with my ass burning from the whipping he'd just given me and even though I could see that both my nipples were surrounded by bruised and sore flesh, I couldn't help but think what a brilliant move that was—to keep me there in that position while he read my folder. I wanted him more desperately than I had anyone else in the room. Sheer admiration made me feel that way.

"No other languages but French—and that's Canadian French," he said with a heavily accented and disappointed voice that I thought would make me cry all over again. But then I felt the weight of his arm as it rested on one shoulder and the pressure of the movement of his other hand as he wrote in the folio.

"You may sit up now," he said when he was done.

I knelt up and nodded to him, hoping to make it something of a bow. He smiled at the attempt and gave one of my nipples a last twist before he moved on.

I was even more confident now that the last two men had both made a notation in my folder. I tried to stop my mind from working that way, but I couldn't fight the desire to be wanted by as many of them as possible, and I couldn't stop thinking that it would be the worst thing of all to be sold for less than the rest of the slaves.

What pride do slaves have other than the approval of our masters? I wondered. And I couldn't think of anything that made any more sense than that.

They continued to make their inspections, stopping at my table and feeling my body, creating waves of suffering as they pinched and pulled at my nipples and defying privacy as their fingers explored my anus and my balls and my cock. There were many who wanted to see my ass dance for their whips and crops and paddles, and I did it all for each one of them. The source of my absurd strength was the feeling of pride every time one more of them wrote in my book, the knowledge that I was wanted.

I couldn't remember how much time passed, and I couldn't keep track of when I was in tears and when I was simply accepting the pain and humiliation as inevitable. By the time the end was drawing closer, I was exhausted; every part of my body ached, if not from beatings and pinches, then from the horrible pain of kneeling on the hard glass.

I should be handsome for these people, but I knew my hair was plastered to my skull with sweat. They should have thought I was appealing, but I could smell the stink from my own perspiration. I could only hope my bruises and my tears were things they found beautiful.

I only wanted it to end—to go with any one of them and to at least know who and what I was going to be living with. The parade of their bodies in their clothes and the smell of their champagne and their cigars had become a huge confusion that I couldn't stand any longer. I wanted to go home—that was my plaintive cry—and it didn't matter what home was, just that I be taken there.

That was when he appeared.

As soon as I looked into his face, I felt a surge of fear and lust course its way through me. He wasn't the largest man I'd seen and in most ways not the most attractive. He was slightly taller than average and dressed, as most of the rest of them had been, in evening clothes. He was dark-haired, and his beard was so heavy that there was a shadow where it would have grown out if he weren't clean-shaven. His eyebrows were dark as well, and his hair was curly. He had blue eyes, so light that they were ominous, for they seemed almost otherworldly and were such a contrast to his deeply tanned complexion.

He simply stood there for a while and studied me. I ran my tongue over my lips at one point; they'd dried out from the tension. He reached forward then, and his finger followed the same route. It was a strangely intimate act in the middle of all the other intimacies I'd endured. I didn't even think about it, but automatically my tongue darted out and met the fingertip, rubbing against his nail's edge.

He enjoyed that. The finger didn't withdraw but instead pressed against my mouth. I sucked it in as soon as I realized what he wanted. Another finger joined it. Then a third. They rested under my tongue at first, just letting me lather them with it. But then the fourth finger came in, and all of them pushed backward, all the way into my throat.

There was no way I could stop gagging; that was beyond my control. But I refused to back away from this eerie invasion. He began to move the hand in and out of the back of my mouth, as though the four fingers were fucking it. I could sense that they were being covered with some fluid of mine more viscous than spit. The surface of his flesh was slippery and seemed to be able to move even more easily after a while.

My face was contorted with pain, and my chest was heaving from the exertion of letting him stay so deep inside me. Finally, though, he withdrew. It wasn't the end of his inspection—I knew it wouldn't be.

He took his wet hand and used my own liquids as extra lubricant to help him explore my ass. I lifted up, straining against the gold chains even more than I had before with the others who'd fucked me that way.

Again, he wasn't satisfied with one finger. He quickly had three inside me and used them savagely, pulling against the edge of my anus, rocking me back and forth with it as a handle. All the time he did that, his other finger and thumb were holding my balls so his palm could press them painfully against my belly. He gave my testicles one last horrible shove, yanked his fingers from my ass, and then stood back.

He didn't have to signal to Stephen; the servant had been there holding the tray with towel and water before it was necessary. He went through the motions and then picked up the folder. He read it and smiled at something or other inside—perhaps comments from my trainer that I hadn't been allowed to read. Then he took a pen from his pocket and wrote on the folder.

When he put it down, he reached over and placed a hand on the side of my head. At first I thought he meant to hit me, but he didn't, he simply held it there. I turned my head into his hand, and he allowed me to nestle my mouth against his palm. I reached out my tongue and licked his flesh, tasting fresh sweat on it, perhaps some of the champagne, but especially, tasting him, the man I hoped would be my master.

5

Montclair

I watched him as he moved up and down the row. I hadn't seen him enter the room, but the progress he made seemed to indicate that I was the first one of the slaves he examined. He went to my left, toward the couple, next. He was more cruel to them than anyone else had been. He pulled on the male's cock while he slapped the woman's groin hard. Then he fingered both of them, reaching down beneath their legs from the front so that the back of his hands rubbed hard against their tender skin.

When he went to examine their chests, he sucked so hard on the man's that the guy had to cry out and beg him to stop—a mistake none of us had made and which was rewarded by a quick and effective gag being roughly shoved into his mouth. He also used a paddle on both their buttocks after having made them bend over and assume the usual position, with their foreheads on the glass table. The sight of him standing behind them and fiercely going at their upraised asses was astonishingly erotic. I imagined myself as part of it—in all ways—as him, the one with the paddle, and as the male, suffering that final humiliation of not only being beaten by another male but also being there helpless while your partner received the violent blows.

They were both quivering with pain and terror by the time he finally moved on.

He disappeared from my view for a while after he was done with them. I was deliriously happy to see that he hadn't written in their folder even after all the attention he'd paid to them. He had gone on farther down the line, and I couldn't quite see to where. In any event, there was something that was going to be much more pressing on my mind.

"Good-looking male," a voice said. The other man had aroused me so much that I'd forgotten that there were more masters to come. I turned quickly and found the black athlete—the first one who'd written in my folio—standing there with another man, the one who'd just spoken.

"I told you so, Jack—just our type."

The new man, Jack, wasn't black; he was Caucasian. But he had the same bulky build as the other, and I suspected immediately they were somehow teammates. Were they lovers as well? *Just our type . . .*

Jack picked up the folder and opened it before he'd even looked me over. He closed it quickly and put it back on the table. Only then did he reach out and begin the humiliating exploration that was now so well practiced—first testing my nipples and then pulling and tugging at my balls, finally inserting his hands in my ass. "I like the hairy chest," Jack admitted. "And the ass is nice." Stephen appeared with the washing tray, and Jack used it. Then he moved around, and I felt one of his big hands grab a cheek of my buttocks.

"Great ass," he said, squeezing it some more. "A shame to have it marked up this way by all the rest of them. It's not even worth seeing how he takes a crop. They've bruised him so much by this time that it wouldn't be a fair test."

I felt another hand take the other side of my ass; it had to be the black athlete's. "Firm, with a nice coating of hair. Solid build. Come on, Jack; you know this guy would do it for us, just what we both like. I'd have this ass of his sitting on my cock every morning, and you could get that mouth whenever you wanted it. We'd have him whenever and however we wanted—including the really rough stuff you like."

"Damned expensive, and Montclair says he's going to bid on him."

"We can afford it together; we can outbid him."

"We'll talk."

Montclair! I knew who they were talking about—the man who'd devastated me so very much. As the two of them walked away, I wanted to call out after them and beg them not to bid, to leave me to Montclair. But I knew better. I'd seen what happened to the one person who'd dared cry out, and I was determined not to do anything that would either bring on that punishment or make the man, Montclair, think less of me.

The display of the slaves was drawing to a close. More and more customers were taking seats in the chairs and couches in front of us. But before any announcement was made, he was back.

He walked by me and stopped in front of Andre. Montclair reached out to touch the coffee-skinned slave in front of him. My heart sank. The other slave was as exhausted as I—he had to be—and his face was swollen with the tears he'd shed from the many beatings and explorations he'd received. But I was still sure I couldn't compete with Andre.

Montclair snapped his fingers for a whip, and Stephen ran over to deliver it. Andre bent over slowly and elegantly; I was sure that I could never have done it as well as he did. Then his powerful thighs and his hard, rounded buttocks were there, lifted up in the air, waiting for the crop to land.

The blows were quick and savage, just as mine had been. Every part of Andre's body shuddered with each one. But it only made him look even more handsome and the muscles even more pronounced. The sweat was pouring down his sides when Montclair was done, and I could see his chest heave with his sobs.

Montclair came to the front and pulled Andre up onto his knees. He ran a hand through the nappy curls of the black man's hair; then suddenly, without warning, he grabbed a handful of it and twisted Andre's head to the side. Andre gasped with pain, but the black man still didn't give in. Then Montclair smiled. He released the slave's hair and picked up his file, writing something in it.

I felt lost. He'd pick Andre; I was sure of it. And I was going to have to go with the two athletes. They would live well, and they would be able to take care of me. I tried to imagine the wonderful things about their well-conditioned bodies, but it did no good. They held out little hope for fantasy, for anything out of the ordinary. What had they said? One would fuck me in the morning, and the other could use my mouth when he wanted it? Perhaps some "rough stuff"—and that was the extent of their imaginations when they were presented with the possibility of owning someone?

I had to confront my desires then. I suddenly understood more about why I'd come there than I'd ever known before. I didn't want to just break with my life at home. I wanted to do one extraordinary thing with my life. I wanted to go all the way with an idea—or I wanted to be taken all the way. I wanted—if only for a while, if only for three years—to live a life without dreams. I wanted to live a life where the most outrageous fantasies and the most frightening nightmares merged with reality so much that I couldn't distinguish any borders. To leave all this at the level of just being a sexual toy for two unimaginative athletes was . . . too little. I didn't want to settle for good sex. I wanted a magician.

"Are we ready to proceed?" It was Cantrell talking. The sounds of the crowd quieted down quickly. "Mr. Montclair, are you finished?" Cantrell must have realized that Montclair hadn't made it to the female at the end of the line yet. But he wasn't interested. He simply waved his agreement and moved to take an open seat that was almost directly in front of Andre—more proof that my compatriot would be chosen over me.

I had been told the sale would be done with silent bids. The men and women who were interested in specific sales had made themselves known with their notations in the files. Now Cantrell moved down the line to the place where the female who was alone waited. He picked up her folder and opened it.

"We will have five bidders on this slave," he announced to the audience. He sent two of his servants running through the crowd to deliver slips of paper on which the bids were to be noted.

"You understand the rules. You may make a single bid, but—for the agreed-upon fee—you may also pay to have the privilege to continue in another round of bidding, if one is necessary. The sum you bid must be in excess of the contracted amount; that's the only rule. We have purposely made the fee for continuing the auction very high, both to discourage picayune offers and distractions and to help cover the costs of The Network, especially the security service in charge of recovering runaways. Now, if those of you who are bidding on this particularly slave will give your papers back to my servants . . ."

Cantrell stood there fondling the woman's bare breasts while the activity went on around the room. He leaned down and whispered something in her ears that brought on a furious blush.

Even while the auction was taking place, I could see other slaves of Cantrell's serving a new round of drinks. They were all dressed in those same purple silk shorts, and it was plain that none of them wore anything underneath. The shirts some had worn earlier were gone, and they were all barechested.

I watched as Peter moved through the crowd with a tray of champagne glasses. *I'll be like him soon,* I thought as I studied the way he bent over to present each glass. But being like him wasn't going to be easy; that was obvious. Because every customer seemed to hold the right to feel his body. He endured countless fingers on his nipples, and whenever a hand wandered to his crotch, his legs opened up, letting the master or mistress explore him as shamelessly as we'd been explored.

He was moving in our direction, toward the end of the room, where Cantrell was now reading the various bids. Peter suddenly saw Montclair, and there was no doubt he knew him. Peter froze and stared at the blue-eyed man with a shocked expression. I wondered what must have gone on between them, and when.

"We have sold our first slave. To the ladies from Montreal." Cantrell's announcement was greeted with a polite round of applause. Stephen and another servant went to work removing the gold chains that had bound the woman, leaving only her collar around her neck.

They lifted her up off the table. Her legs were stiff—I could understand that—and she moved awkwardly at first. But Stephen quickly had a leash attached to the collar and had pushed her roughly to the floor, on her hands and knees. *So that's how we'll all be delivered,* I realized as I watched Stephen and the other servant slap the female's buttocks and force her to move quickly across the floor to the two mistresses.

They took their delivery graciously, obviously pleased with the young woman. They had her kneel in between them while they grabbed at her and explored her all over again, as though for the first time. She was panicked, looking first to one and then to the other as their hands kept moving over her body.

"And now," Cantrell said, bringing everyone's attention

back to the auction, "our next slave." He stood in front of Andre and opened the young black man's folio. Cantrell raised an eyebrow in surprise. "There will be . . . fifteen bids for this male."

A murmur went through the audience that was so loud, it was obvious that this was unusual. It only depressed me further, since only eight people had written in my book.

The slips of paper were delivered by the servants. I watched them move around the room, many of them grabbed at by members of The Network, who obviously enjoyed the easy examination of Cantrell's slaves. But I also saw that Peter had moved closer to Montclair as he continued his rounds.

Montclair was watching him now. There was a smirk on his face, one so obvious and so intent that I knew he had also recognized Peter. He was simply waiting for the big man to arrive near him.

The slips of paper were returned to Cantrell just as Peter reached Montclair. The half-naked servant bent over and offered Montclair the tray of drinks. The master whispered something in his ear, and Peter seemed to go pale all at once. He put down his tray and then stood up. He lowered his short pants to his knees and stood there, obviously complying with the order to exhibit himself.

This was the first time I'd seen the cock that I'd held in the dressing room. It was thick, though not as long as I would have thought. What I hadn't noticed—I hadn't had time because of Stephen's interruption—was how very large Peter's balls were and how very low they hung down from his body.

Montclair reached over and lifted them up, as though he were examining them carefully. There was so much skin on Peter's balls that Montclair could actually make them swing back and forth when he dropped them. He waved Peter away after that, leaving the servant with his shorts still around his knees. Peter was blushing angrily as he pulled the pants back up and continued his rounds.

"There have been five guaranteed bids for this slave," Cantrell announced after having read them. The crowd didn't just murmur now; it was obvious that five people paying what must be the large fee in order to be able to bid a second time was even more unusual than the large number of initial bidders. The crowd began to talk loudly, swept up in the excitement of the event.

Again servants were sent running through the crowd. Montclair got one of the new slips of paper—still another bad sign for my hopes that he'd buy me.

This time, though, when the bids were read by Cantrell, there was no more suspense. "Mr. Montclair." Cantrell bowed toward the smiling master and clapped his hands. I watched as Andre was removed from his bondage and thrown onto his hands and knees. Stephen was the one to urge him to crawl faster as he was sent over to Montclair.

I watched the whole scene with burning jealousy. *I wanted to be there!* I wanted to be the one he'd chosen. I slumped back on my haunches as I watched Andre's head move into the middle of Montclair's lap.

But there wasn't any time to relax. I was next. A sudden wave of nausea rushed through me as Cantrell came up beside me. I tried to jump against my bondage when his hand rested on my shoulder. "Another single male"—Cantrell picked up my folder and then continued his announcement—"for whom eight people have expressed the desire to bid."

There was another flow of sweat from my body, but this time it seemed cold against my hot flesh. I felt a new and totally different desire to cry. This time, it wouldn't be from pain but from the shock of what I was doing. My mind raced back and tried to remember the other ways I'd thought about all this—the pride that had sometimes come to the fore of my thoughts or the sense of excitement. But I couldn't find them; I was too stunned that I was really doing this, now, here, at this very moment.

I watched Montclair fill out his slip of paper but couldn't become excited or hopeful. Certainly he was just going through the motions and wouldn't buy two men at once.

"You're going to be very happy in your slavery, Timothy." Cantrell was talking to me softly while the bids were collected. "Your trainer, whom I admire so very much, thinks you are a natural to it. Who knows, you may well be back here in three years, on the block again, and perhaps I'll bid on you myself then. I like my males to be more seasoned than you are, but there are many here who'll value the reports of your enthusiasm."

Enthusiasm. So that's what he'd said about me. And maybe it was the right word, or it had been at one time. If only Montclair could be my master, it would be again.

The slips were delivered, and I watched with a mixture of dread and disbelief as Cantrell opened and read the notes that would decide my life. "There are three guaranteed bids," he announced.

He handed three more pieces of paper to servants, who went to deliver them. I found some solace in at least having a second round in the bidding. And then I saw one of them being delivered to Montclair! He was still bidding for me. I searched the rest of the room and saw another piece of paper delivered to the two athletes. I lost track of the third.

Montclair could still buy me! The slips were filled out quickly and were returned to Cantrell. He was surprised by the results. "The round of bidding is negated. All three members of the audience have once again guaranteed their bids. I will write the highest bid on the new ballots, and that must be the floor for the next round."

The ballots were marked and returned to the bidders. The athletes looked at me and talked to one another again. Montclair didn't hesitate, but wrote something quickly. This time I saw that the third ballot went to the blond foreigner.

Him! If I couldn't have Montclair, then I wanted him. At

least there would be something more there. I watched him and stared back at his eyes as he continued to study me. Please! I tried to calm down, tried to remind myself of his cruelty, but I only thought now about how handsome he was and how quickly and surely he'd taken control. . . .

The bids were in Cantrell's hands once again. "Again, all three bids are guaranteed." The crowd was openly astonished now—and so was I. Montclair was still a part of it. "The rules declare that, for the next round, all the bidders must double their promised fee to The Network."

Once again, Cantrell sent the servants out. I watched as the athletes made out their slip and the other two followed suit.

The bids were delivered to Cantrell. I waited. I closed my eyes and prayed that this would be the end. "Mr. Montclair."

The crowd was taken aback by the announcement. I opened my eyes and stared at Montclair and at Andre, both of them smiling at me, but each with a very different kind of expression to accompany that smile. I didn't have time to wonder about that. Stephen and another servant were at my side. After their delay, the crowd finally reacted, and I heard one man call out, "Brilliant buy, the perfect matched pair." Then a woman: "Superbly done, Montclair."

But then Stephen's strong arms were lifting me up. My legs were shot with pain to finally be let free of their cramped torture, and I was forced down on the floor. The gold chain was taken from my wrists next; then, quickly, I could feel Stephen attaching something to my neck chain. A sharp slap on my ass sent me across the carpet toward Montclair, my new master, and Andre, my companion for the next three years.

I couldn't see where I was going; the leash was being pulled too quickly for me to get my bearings. But there were legs and feet flashing in front of my vision. Hands reached out and grabbed parts of my body; one took a painful hold of my balls and tugged at them even while Stephen was forcing me forward, away from that grip.

Then, suddenly, there was Andre's handsome body and skin, right beside me, and in front of me the waiting crotch of Montclair, the man who had just purchased me. His hand came out and stayed still in front of my face. I knew what it wanted. I reached forward and kissed it. Then the hand reached up and tousled my hair and gently pulled me in even closer, till my face was rubbing against his crotch. I could feel the hardening cock inside it. Andre was being moved up with me, and we were both pressing our naked bodies against one another while our heads were being forced against the master's cock.

6

A Trio

"Don't say a word," Montclair said. He used his hands to reposition us to face front, toward the auction, on our knees. It was a great relief, and I couldn't help sighing. He kept a hand on one of my shoulders, and I could see that the other was on Andre.

The black man looked over at me slyly and winked. He reached down and took my own hand and held it. We were going to do this together.

We both relaxed back on our haunches, resting against our master's thighs.

Our master's thighs . . .

Montclair owned us. Montclair was our master. We were his slaves. Those were the only truths we knew at that moment in time. But they were enormous realities.

We were able to stay there and watch the rest of it. The spectacle of the auction from this viewpoint was just as unreal. It was so amazing that I forgot the burning skin on my ass and the painful points of my nipples. All of those sensations and the memory of myself up on the now-empty table disappeared in the midst of my fascination with the sale.

The auction went on for another hour. The couple took the most time. I didn't care that they had more original bids than I did. I was satisfied that they had fewer than Andre and that they had gone through fewer rounds than I had. Somehow it secured our position as the stars of the event, and that was important to me.

And what was much more interesting was watching their faces and their bodies. Had I been so obvious when I was being sold?

The male of the couple seemed to be trying to talk even though the gag was still in his mouth, making speech impossible. The woman was totally submissive; I could tell by her slouch and by the way her eyes looked straight down toward the floor. Cantrell stood behind them and seemed to reward the woman by calmly running his hands over her back while at the same time he only goaded the male by reaching in front to pull on his cock and balls and elicit even more physical reactions for the crowd's entertainment.

I heard some of the audience's comments. They weren't spoken very loudly, but the people who sat around us made their impressions of the couple on the table perfectly clear: "She's much stronger than he is; he'd only he trouble." "Better to let one of those men who enjoy breaking that kind of rebellion take him. He'd be a waste of time to anyone who wanted service." "I imagine she talked him into it. It's always so dangerous to take on a couple; there are so many dynamics that are their own, so much history they bring into their new life, that it's seldom worth it." "Unless you enjoy watching it all unfold and unless you wish the special pleasure of a male being humiliated in front of the woman who was once his." "Don't be so presumptuous! She could have been the mistress in their life!"

I couldn't make out just who was speaking to whom. I didn't dare turn my head so much that my interest would be noticeable. And besides, there was the rest of the sale to watch.

The couple were bought by someone I couldn't see; he was sitting far over in the other corner. That left only Gene. The blond man stiffened when that same realization struck him.

His hair, which had been so well styled back in the preparation room, was stringy with sweat now. His pale skin made the welts from the trial beatings appear exaggerated. I knew that my own flesh—bruised as it was—didn't have the dark red lines that Gene's showed.

As soon as Cantrell approached him, Gene's cock got stiffly erect—something that brought on laughs and even some applause from the audience. No matter how anxious he appeared to be when he looked up at the auctioneer, that erection was a greater truth; there was no doubt in their minds.

The sale went quickly. I was amazed by it all as I watched the runners moving once again through the audience. *A person is being sold*... And he had a name—Gene—that I'd heard. He had a history that I didn't know about; he hadn't joined in when Andre and I told our stories. Who was he? How did he ever get here?

Cantrell announced the winner, and I saw Gene's tall blond body being dragged off the table. I relived the painful stretching that I'd experienced myself when my legs had finally been released from their bondage and Stephen had led me, collared and leashed, through the crowd to my new master.

As though he wanted to remind me of that very moment, Montclair reached down and put his hand on the back of my neck. I couldn't help but respond and rubbed my head against it. That seemed to be something he enjoyed; he patted my shoulder, and a sudden shock of pleasure went through me as I realized I had pleased my new master for the first time.

Then it was over. The crowd began to mill around and talk as easily and inconsequentially as if they had simply watched a movie together. More than a few came over and talked to Montclair, most of them to compliment him on choosing the two of us. The same terms I'd heard earlier were being used again: "A matched pair." "A fine combination." Andre only held my hand tighter.

I was surprised that we stayed there so long. Even now, as other guests were beginning to depart, Montclair kept his seat. The others who'd bought slaves were the first to leave, it seemed, probably wanting to get their new charges home and into use at once. But Montclair didn't move.

I wanted to see him more clearly but couldn't so long as he kept us facing front. I certainly hadn't seen much of him earlier, when we had been on our hands and knees, our faces buried in his crotch. I had to satisfy myself with Andre—which was no problem.

He had to have been as proud as I was. As the people would come by and make their comments, both of our cocks fell forward in half-hard arcs, as though we wanted to show them off to our master's friends.

We soon enough got to see why Montclair was staying around. Peter came by with another of his trays of champagne and offered one to our master again. "Peter, what do you think of my new toys?" Montclair asked.

Peter seemed to freeze. "I hope you enjoy them, sir."

"Have you any words of wisdom for them, Peter?"

"Sir?" Peter was obviously unsure of what he was supposed to say—or what would be safe to say.

"You've been in The Network for quite some time, I hear. Certainly you have something that you could tell them that will make their servitude more . . . beneficial, haven't you? Certainly your experience must have provided you with some insights, some suggestion."

Peter stood and took a while before he answered. "To love the master's whip, sir."

"Really? Do you love your master's whip now, Peter?"

There was another hesitation, "A slave has no choice, sir."

"Go and get a whip, Peter."

He put the tray down and moved over to where the slaves

had been displayed for the auction. He looked around the area and finally picked up a riding crop and brought it back.

"You two," Montclair said to us, "turn back around on your hands and knees." We both moved quickly. "How is that, Peter? Did they do it well enough?"

"No, sir. Their legs are too close together; their master may want their thighs."

"You heard the expert," Montclair leaned over and said to us. "Spread your legs apart more."

We hurried to do what we'd been told. The new posture was even more humiliating. It left my balls hanging loosely, and I immediately began to worry that when the beating began, he'd hit them—accidentally or on purpose.

"Better, Peter?" Montclair asked.

"Yes, sir."

"Then why don't you show them the kind of whipping they can learn to love."

"I . . . I can't, sir."

"Why not?"

"I don't mean any disrespect at all, Mr. Montclair, but I can't show them what you want. That would have to come directly from their master. Another slave's whipping them can only be punishment—and usually the worst kind."

"What a good answer, Peter," Montclair said. I could sense him leaning back in his chair. "That's a much better answer than I ever expected to hear from you." Montclair was reaching for something. Then, after a moment, he handed it to Peter. "Take this to your master. I'll be waiting for his reply."

"Back on your knees," Montclair said to us.

It took a while before Peter returned and handed something to Montclair. "Yes, fine," he said. "You," Montclair called out to Stephen, who was passing by, "come here."

"Sir." Stephen stood in front of Montclair and waited to hear what it was he wanted.

"Take these shorts from this servant and return them to your master. I've only purchased the man, not his clothing."

Peter opened his mouth as though he wanted to protest whatever it was that was going on, but Stephen seemed to know better than to question any of the orders of the people in The Network and moved toward his former compatriot. Stephen reached for Peter's shorts and pulled at them. Peter didn't resist, but he didn't help Stephen, either. He simply stood there, as though in shock.

"Join my new toys, Peter," Montclair said. "You're going to have many opportunities to teach them all those valuable lessons of yours."

"But, sir . . ." Peter seemed to understand that he shouldn't speak, but the words came out, anyhow, as though they were simply escaping rather than being spoken consciously.

"I bought you; it's as simple as that," Montclair said, evidently willing to forgive the transgression. "I made your master a very interesting offer, one I knew he wouldn't refuse. I have assumed your contract."

Montclair turned to Stephen again. "Go and get my men; they're waiting for me downstairs. Tell them I'm ready and they should bring equipment for three new slaves." Then Montclair returned to Peter. "I told you, kneel with these other two. You belong with them."

7

The Lawn

"Get up!"

"Now! "

"Wake up!"

The yelling voices dragged me awake. There were rough hands pulling at the restraints that held my wrists and ankles, and I was being brutally turned over and around until my chest was across the cot where I'd slept and my knees were on the ground. My sleepiness still muffled some of the reality of what was happening.

"Spread your legs apart!" Booted feet kicked at my knees repeatedly until I'd separated them as far as I could. I tried to kneel up to see who was doing this to me, but a strong arm pushed me back down. "Stay where you are!" he yelled.

Other voices were screaming the same orders around the room; they must be doing the same things to Andre and to Peter. I somehow got that thought into my conscious mind. My eyes were still only half-focused. I couldn't make out all the things that were happening around me.

But then there were clothed legs kneeling behind me, coming in between my naked thighs. The cold tip of a hard, condom-covered cock was poking between my ass cheeks. I tried to rise up again, and the arms shoved me back down once more. "Fight it and I'll give you the whipping of your life."

The cock fucked all the way into me with one thrust. I fought against the forearm that was braced against my back, but it was no use, and soon the hard cock was pounding in and out of my ass with long, rocking motions.

I gave in to it, the sensations turning into a humiliating pleasure much more quickly than I'd ever expected they could. I relaxed my muscles and let my chest go flat against the cot's mattress.

I was still half-asleep; I didn't have use of my full consciousness to resist what was happening and could only respond to the pleasure of his cock. It felt so immense while it was so deep inside me.

"Good, you're going to be real good at this," the voice said behind me. "This is the way Mr. Montclair likes you all to wake up in the morning. It's part of being owned by him, getting a good fuck to start your day. You'll learn to like it even better. You'll see; you'll love it."

His voice was thick with sexual excitement; he seemed to be turning himself on just by talking to me. The thrusts got harder and came more quickly, and so did his breathing. "Yes, you're going to learn to love it."

Then I could feel his pubic hair press against my ass one last time as his muscles went stiff and his voice turned into a grunting groan. He collapsed on my back and stayed there, his cock still inside me, for a moment longer.

He pulled out so quickly that there was a stabbing pain in my anus when the erection left it. I could hear other voices in the room speaking as softly as he had spoken to me and, quickly after that, two more loud roars announcing two more orgasms.

Then the body was behind me again, pulling me backward, up on to my knees. "There's another part to this little ritual, something else Mr. Montclair likes to have happen every morning." A calloused hand had gripped hold of my own erection. The hand was covered with grease, probably the same he'd used to fuck me, I realized. He began to pump on my cock.

"Mr. Montclair likes to start your day off right, you see, show you what's up—that's not just a dick up your ass; he wants you to shoot, too—so come on, get hard and ready."

While he was pumping away at my cock, his free hand came around and ran over my chest until it found one of my nipples and began to twist it. The slightest contact was painful, the tit was still sore from the work it had received at the auction last night. I yelled out as soon as he started to pinch and pull at it.

"Don't give me any trouble," he warned. "You're not in any position to make complaints." The hand kept mauling my chest. It left the one nipple alone for a brief moment of relief and then grabbed hold of the other, twisting it even more painfully.

"This is what you're going to be getting for three years; you might as well accept it." The other hand was still pumping at my cock.

This is what you're going to be getting for three years . . . The thought repeated itself over and over again in my mind—this was what it was going to be. Not Montclair but faceless fucks. No mysterious love I could only experience, never understand, just constant abuse. I tried to remember some of the fear and loathing I'd felt yesterday—had it really only been yesterday?—but I couldn't. I could only feel the emptiness where the cock had been in my ass and the violent sensations of my own erection as it was being stroked faster and faster. I was a slave. I was bought, I was in the hands of my masters. . . . *This is what you're going to be getting for three years. . . .*

The orgasm came on me without my ever even noticing it. It just erupted, the waves of come flowed out of my cock and hit the side of the cot in thick, pulsing waves.

I collapsed forward again. I didn't have time to even catch up with my breathing before a leather collar was roughly attached to my neck. A leash pulled on it and forced me to move backward, away from the cot. I was being dragged off, still confused, still not understanding what this was all about.

A lash came down sharply on my ass. "Stay on your hands and knees! Move it! This way! Come on!" The lash bit out again and caught my ass once more; this time the tip grazed against my balls, and I yelped in pain. "Shut up and move it!" the voice commanded. I raced to follow its denim-clad legs and its leather boots as it led me out of the room.

"Got some food for them." I had never heard the voice before.

"Okay, come on over here; your lunch is served." The order came from the man who'd fucked me this morning and then led me out here to the lawn.

The three of us scurried over toward him and arrived at the huge bowl that sat by his feet.

"Go to it," the voice said.

We didn't hesitate the way we had this morning when we'd been given breakfast. We dove into the bowl, not paying any attention to our faces rubbing against each other as we ate.

Peter and Andre must have been as starved as I was, and seeing how they went after the bits of melon that were there, they were just as thirsty. We hadn't been allowed to stop or slow down the whole morning—not even for a drink of water. My throat was so parched, it was sore, and the wet pieces of the different melons I could capture with my tongue were pure luxury as they slid into my stomach.

Andre had been the one to make the mistake of trying to eat with his hands at breakfast, and he'd paid for it with a lashing. We weren't taking any chances of another, not after the way our asses and shoulders had been beaten all morning.

We'd been on our hands and knees, collared and leashed, since we woke up. We'd been fed hot grain cereal from a communal bowl and then immediately brought outdoors. We were each given a small trowel and put to work weeding the seemingly endless lawns.

No one had spoken to us except to give out the curt orders—always delivered with a slash of the length of leather the different overseers carried. "Open your legs! Don't let them touch one another!" "Don't sit up! Stay on all fours!" "Don't stop working! You're not on a holiday!"

It hadn't even been twenty-four hours since I'd presented myself to Cantrell in his house, and now I was already stripped of anything close to pride as I slurped up the juices at the bottom of the bowl, feeling Andre's own tongue moving against mine.

There were other things in the bowl besides the melon: fresh fruits and vegetables, all of them cut into small enough pieces that we could easily eat them; none of them were cooked, and the crisp broccoli florets were a strange contrast to the soft slices of peach. But it was delicious, perhaps the most delicious meal I'd had in my life.

"Better give 'em a chance to digest all that. Shit, they ate it in no time flat." That was the stranger's voice talking.

"Rest won't do them any good. But Montclair thinks they should have some time on their backs, he wants to make sure they don't just get the sun on one side." He had said all that in a conversational tone. But then he changed back to the brusque manner he used when talking to us, as though we wouldn't even understand him if he didn't: "Go back over there; take a little nap with your bellies up. Mr. Montclair doesn't like it if you're not nicely developed here."

Peter, Andre, and I moved more slowly back toward the

center of the area where we'd been working and gratefully sprawled out for a rest. The too-familiar sound of the lash made me jerk myself back to being fully alert. It had landed on Andre's belly. "I did *not* tell you you could put your legs together. Spread them out—and your arms, too, up above your head."

All three of us immediately did what we'd been told to do. The vulnerable posture was nothing—it was rest, something we'd had none of.

That damn lash had been in near-constant use, punishing us for being lazy or for trying to hide our balls from view or just to tell us to move this way or that. It didn't help to know it wasn't a vicious instrument; it was light compared to the crops and paddles that had been used at the sale. It stung more than it hurt. But the sting and the never-ending reminder that it was there to be used on us were always there.

But now we could rest. I felt the soft summer breeze rifling through my chest hair and the hair under my arms. It was the first time in hours that I could simply feel the world around me and enjoy it in any way. I took a deep breath and, as soon as I did, had to fight off the urge to cry. I was scared. This wasn't anything like what I'd expected. I had been prepared for so much, but not this relentless labor.

"Any of them chosen yet?" Still a new voice was talking.

Chosen? I wanted to look and see who was speaking and was trying to figure out what that meant but didn't dare.

"No, not yet. You're the first; take your pick. That black one's got great legs; bet he'd throw a mean fuck."

"Yeah. But that little hairy-chested number . . . That looks pretty good to me. Got a good ass on him?"

"You think Montclair would buy him if he didn't?"

The two of them laughed at that. Then I could sense a body moving toward me. It blocked the sun that had been shining in my face. I stared up at him, this man who appeared to be so enormous from where I was as he towered over me with one foot on either side of my chest.

He crouched down so that his knees were on the side of my face. "Yeah, you're pretty good-looking, all right. Not bad at all." His hand came out, and he ran his fingers through my hair. "I got something to show you." He moved his hand away from me and opened his fly. Then he reached into his pants.

He was very handsome, with reddish hair and blue eyes and a deeply tanned face. He was dressed, as the others had been, in jeans and a T-shirt. I watched as he brought out a thick, short cock and large balls. They were topped by light red pubic hair. He stroked his cock and moved forward so that it was hanging inches in front of my face.

It began to grow thicker as he continued to play with it. I was hypnotized by it as I watched it and its pale skin and deep purple veins so close to me. Finally, it was fully erect. It still wasn't very long, but it was certainly very wide. I didn't know if I was supposed to suck it or not, and I was frustrated all over again because I wanted to.

"I just thought you'd like to take a look at this dick," he said with a friendly smile. "It's going to be the one to wake you up tomorrow. I figured if you got a chance to look at it now, you'd appreciate it all the more in the morning. This'll give you a chance to dream about it tonight."

With that, he stood up and gave his cock one last stroke before he shoved it into his pants. He slowly zipped up and left me there.

"Sir, please!" Andre begged when the lash hit him on the back.

"I told you, don't sit up!" the voice said.

"I . . . I have to piss," Andre said plaintively.

"I'm not stopping you. I'm just telling you not to stop working. You got to piss—piss."

I kept moving over the lawn, digging up the weeds and putting them in one of the baskets that each of us was dragging along beside him. But I was totally involved with what was happening to Andre.

He tried to hold it for a long time, but I could hear first a trickle and then the entire flow of his bladder loosening and his wetting the lawn he was crawling over.

The sound was hypnotic—and contagious. My own body began to rebel at the discipline I'd kept it under. The sound of Andre's piss was too great a seduction. I felt myself lose control, and then my cock was spilling out a steady stream of the warm liquid, right on to the spot I'd have to move over soon.

No one said a word about it. The three of us kept on working, desperate to keep that lash away from our bodies.

"Back to work!" The lash snapped at my hips, and I jumped to my knees and fell forward onto my hands to stop it from striking again. I'd forgotten and stopped to wipe the sweat from my forehead. I quickly found my trowel and returned to my task of searching for weeds in the lawn.

Two more men came by that afternoon and asked the overseer which of us were available. One chose Andre, and the other was told that only Peter was free. Both of them repeated a ritual similar to the one the redhead had performed with me, displaying a hard cock to the slave he was going to fuck awake in the morning.

The work went on and on. It wasn't until the sun was starting to set that we were fed once again—more fruit and vegetables, this time with cubes of cheese included. We were exhausted, but the overseer made no allowance for that. He used the lash to drive us back toward the place where we'd slept last night.

Andre was crying by the time we got there. It wasn't just the pain; I was sure of that. The sun had been hot, and I could feel the tightness that let me know a sunburn was coming on, but neither that nor the lash was enough to make him cry. It was the fatigue, the terrible tiredness. Every part of my own body ached, and even if he was better developed than I, I knew that Andre's muscles were just as sore from the unfamiliar actions we'd been forced to use and by the lack of any rest. I had napped during the lunch break and couldn't know how long it took, but I was sure it hadn't been more than an hour.

The overseer stopped us outside the open door of the small building. "Got to wash you up," the voice said. There was a sudden slack in the leash that had been directing me, and I knew he had dropped it. "Now, don't get any ideas about moving around. We're not wasting hot water on the three of you, but if you move away, I swear I'll take the skin off your butts."

Then there was a sudden sound of a hose being turned on and the awful shock of the torrent of cold water as it hit my hot and bruised body. I screamed out loud, but didn't dare move. Andre and Peter both yelled when the stream of water was directed toward them. The overseer only laughed out loud.

After a few minutes I was at least able to make my body accept what was happening. The overseer moved forward, and the water was directed at my hair, under my belly, on my cock and balls, and even in the crack of my ass. He went through all of that with the other two.

Then it was over. I breathed deeply that it was done and felt him pick up the leash once more. "Inside. Come on, get a move on."

We went across the transom and into the small room. There were three cots in a row where we had slept last night. That was all. There was no other furniture and no other facilities.

I had only been aware of the one overseer, but now there were more bodies surrounding us and lifting us up onto the bed. As we were last night, we were put into bondage, our wrists and ankles pulled to the extreme corners of the beds.

I tried to see who the men were, tried to find something individual about them, but they moved too quickly, and the times they touched me were too mechanical to let me capture anything about them. They were gone in minutes, turning out the lights before they left and leaving us only in the dying dusk of the evening.

"Peter," Andre said from the other side of the room. "What's this about? What are they doing to us? Why?"

"It doesn't help to know what they're doing," Peter answered.

"But I want to know." Andre sounded desperate. "You're the one who's been here before, who understands them. What are they doing to us?"

"They're making it so bad, we'll forget they caused it and only be happy it's finished. They're making it so horrible that when they do the smallest thing for us, we'll be grateful. But it doesn't help to know that! It doesn't help at all. . . ." His voiced eased away, and I knew he'd fallen into a deep sleep.

I could hear Andre's own soft sleeping sounds soon after that. I wasn't going to be able to stay awake much longer, either. But I tried to force myself. I was thinking about that red-crowned cock that was going to fuck me in the morning. The last thing I remembered were the purple veins that wove themselves around the blunt stalk of the redhead's cock. It was going to be inside me when I woke up. . . .

8

Red

"Time to get up!" The screaming started again the next morning. "Move it!" "Wake up!" There was a chorus of them again, and again I was barely awake enough to understand that the restraints were being removed from my wrists and ankles.

I shook my head, trying to force myself to become conscious. *Where was I? What was going on?*

Hands were moving me around to put me on the floor, on my knees, facing the cot where I'd slept. I remembered this from yesterday and immediately went stiff with fear.

"Hey, now, don't you remember what you got coming this morning?" The voice that was whispering in my ear wasn't one of those that was still yelling at the others. And his hands, tightly gripping me at the waist as he guided me to lean over onto the cot, weren't slapping me the way others were beating Andre and Peter.

"I told you I'd be here," the redheaded man was saying to me. "I told you you should dream about it."

And I had. All the images from last night flooded my mind as I remembered my visions of his cock. I calmed down immediately; something told me I was safe in his arms.

I listened as the man I was already calling Red in my mind leaned back a little and tore something open. Then there was another sound of a jar being unscrewed. I knew he had put on a condom and now was greasing up his cock.

He leaned forward, and the blunt end of his thick erection was pressing itself against me, then it slid up the crack of my ass. "Now we're going to have a real good morning together, a nice wake-up . . ."

He reached down and repositioned his erection so that its tip was directly in front of my hole. He shoved once, and the wide end pushed into me. I didn't even think before I moved backward, letting my motion force the whole of it inside me.

"Hey, you're good," he said with a raspy voice. "You have real potential," he teased. Then he began to rock back and forth, letting the cock fuck me with slow and even motions.

He didn't wait till he was done to get to my own cock. He reached around and took hold of it while he was still inside. He held it and let the rocking jerk me off in his fist. I came first, loudly and with a violence I hadn't felt with sex in a long time. It was one of those orgasms that left me breathless and spent even as he kept on pumping at my ass. When he was finished, he moved out gently and stood up. He reached down and ran a hand through my hair.

In a minute there was a new set of hands on me, attaching that damn leash to my collar and jerking me back down on the floor. "Come on, *move!* Get *going!*" And I was dragged off toward our breakfast.

Someday it had to end. We knew that. But we had no idea when.

Every morning was the same: We were dragged out of our sound sleep, fucked and jerked off, then led to the bowl, where we ate cereal.

We spent every day working. It was usually on the lawn, though sometimes they'd take us into a large garden to weed there. It was always spent on our hands and knees, and it was always done with the omnipresent reality of the lash.

We'd be fed about noon. Around that time, three men would appear, and we would be introduced to the cock that was going to fuck us the next day.

After we were finished working, we'd be hosed down and then secured to our cots. We never had the energy for any real conversation. Andre and I begged Peter for help, information, anything that would make this easier to accept, but he couldn't really help us at all. He'd be as tired as we were, and whatever was happening to us wasn't something he really understood beyond the simple message he'd given us that first night: that we'd love them when the whip stopped.

But I had a secret that I didn't dare share with them. I already loved one of the others: Red. I held the memory of that second morning in my mind as though it were the one thing that would keep my sanity through it all. The others could fuck me, whip me as I labored in their fields, and they could make sure I didn't have the least bit of dignity in my entire existence with them. But I had the vision of Red in my mind. He'd return. And when he did . . . I would be so good to him that he would have to notice.

We began to be able to identify the overseers. There wasn't as large a number of them as there were other men who'd come and go with the food or for the morning sex. The one we hated the most was a blond. He was the only one who seemed to want to use the lash for simple enjoyment. When we heard his voice and its distinctive southern accent, we immediately tightened our muscles in preparation for the abuse we knew would be coming.

Another overseer was black. He was as large and as powerfully built as the athlete who'd wanted to buy me. He was never senselessly cruel. But he also didn't know just how strong he could be and often used the lash more severely than the others did. He was also the one who enjoyed our bodies the most. He was the only overseer who'd grab us by the balls and let his fingers slip into our asses. He seemed to do it only when there was no one else around, and I was sure it was something he wasn't supposed to be doing. The small image that there was anything forbidden in this of all places—and that it was happening to us—made his touches even more exciting.

The days merged, one into the next, and I was frightened I would even lose count of how many of them there were. Ten? Twelve? They were all alike, a brutal awakening, a quick fuck and a strange hand masturbating me, working in the hot sun, only a perfunctory cleaning with the cold-water hose, and then desperately needed sleep.

Andre, Peter, and I somehow were making it through. If Peter couldn't explain much to us at night, the quickly whispered conversations we did share gave us some joint strength, some communal support to continue. This had to end; we knew this would have to end. . . .

Then he came back. Red. I was working on a row of vegetables; my beard was long and scratchy—we hadn't been shaved since we'd arrived—and my sweat seemed even more sour than usual on that day. The insects that hovered around me and the humidity made me feel even dirtier, raunchier, than before.

"I wonder how good you still look under all that shit?" the voice said. I jerked my head up to see him there. He was smiling, those blue eyes sparkling in the bright sun. I looked down at the dirt that was caked over my skin and clumped in my chest and pubic hair and felt more miserable than ever before that he'd see me like this.

He crouched down beside me, and his hand reached around to slip a finger in my parted ass, still lubricated from my morning fuck. "But this sure still looks good."

I felt tears running down my face. He reached up his other

hand and wiped one out of the way. "You're not giving in, are you? Don't you have more stuff than this?"

"Yes!" I said that one word more vehemently than any other I'd spoken since I'd arrived here. "Sir, I have more stuff than that."

His finger was still inside me, moving gently around, enticing my cock to a full erection. "That's a good sign." He took the finger out, and I started to cry again. I wanted it back again. I'd thought about him for so long. . . .

He stood up and undid his pants. He pulled out the same pale cock with those purple veins and let it arc out from his body. I didn't wait for him to say anything. I leaned forward and put my lips right at the tip, twisting my head to do it.

The cock seemed to jerk at the contact. I moved backward and watched it well up to its erection. "Remember it?"

"Yes, sir."

"You get it in the morning. Think about that. This old friend of yours will come back then, just like before."

"Wake up." The voice in my ear was soft and seductive. "Time to get that pretty ass out of bed."

My eyes flew open. Morning! I waited for the daily attack. But there wasn't one, and there were no sounds that Andre and Peter were getting the usual treatment, either.

Instead, Red's hands were undoing the restraints on my wrists. "Now listen to me," he said as he worked on the buckles. "This doesn't mean everything's over. Not at all. I know how to use that whip as good as the rest of them. You remember that or I'll have to prove it to you.

"But you can walk today. And we're going to clean you up a bit, too. But when you don't have a good reason to be on your feet, kneel. And when you kneel, keep those legs of yours spread apart so I can see your pretty balls hanging down."

He moved to my ankles and started to release those. "I have to keep you tied up some; don't worry about it, though. And whatever else you do, don't touch your own cock. They must have told you that already, didn't they? That's the cardinal rule here, the slaves can't touch themselves. You understand."

"Yes, sir," I said, not quite believing this was happening, waiting for something to prove to me that it was just the continuation of one of my dreams about him.

His hands reached down to guide me to my feet. I was stiff and unconsciously stretched when I was upright. He gently put my hands behind my back, and I could feel metal cuffs close around both of them.

I saw that both Peter and Andre were getting the same gentle guidance from two of the men I'd seen come to fuck them mornings. Peter was being attended to by a burly-looking bearded man who was the oldest of all of us in the room. He might have been about forty. Andre's wrists were being cuffed by the youngest, a very attractive, clean-shaven man with brown hair.

"Come on; let's get you cleaned up," Red said. He took me by the elbow and walked me out of the hut. The rest of them followed.

Just the fact of walking upright was amazing. I looked down at the thick crusts of dirt and grime on my knees and on my feet as I made my way over the manicured lawn. I was able to look around much more carefully than ever before. There was the large house I'd seen some days, a contemporary-style building that sat up on top of the hill. I knew it had to be Montclair's house. There were other, much smaller buildings clustered around the grounds, some of them no larger than the hut we'd been sleeping in and all of them much closer to the main house.

Probably the most amazing thing of all was the nonchalant way that the few other people we saw reacted to us—three naked men, filthy and handcuffed, walking with their masters. Occasionally, someone would say hello to one or another of our guards, but just as often they would only wave or take no notice at all.

They took us to one of the other buildings. Inside was a huge tiled shower room, something you might find in a well-equipped dormitory. It wasn't as sparse as the servants' quarters at Cantrell's; this place had stalls for the toilets at least.

Red worked a key in the handcuffs and undid them. He went to one of the many small lockers that lined the room and took out a bar of soap, a washcloth, and a small plastic container of shampoo. He handed them to me and, smiling again, nodded to the shower.

The warm water was one of the most luxurious sensations I'd ever known. I let it cascade down over me endlessly as I lathered my body over and over again. I used the cloth to scrub those places where the dirt was most embedded. My knees and hands were raw by the time I was finished, but the sense of cleanliness was so welcome, I didn't care about anything else.

The three other men stood outside the shower area and seemed to talk easily among themselves as they watched us. I could tell they were commenting on us and our bodies by the way they would all stare at one of us all at once. They seemed to be making small comparisons between us.

We must have looked good after the first layer of dirt had been washed away. We'd all lost weight, and our bodies—still muscular—were even sleeker than before. We were all darkly and evenly tanned, Andre the most, of course, but Peter and I had no line left where our bodies had once been protected by bathing suits or other clothes.

And we were happy. The three onlookers had to see how very happy we were. Once we realized that we were honestly and truly going to be given a reprieve, we began to joke with one another. We fell into a total trust for these three men—

never once thinking that might be foolish—and started to giggle talking about our individual saviors; that's just what we thought they were.

Peter's statement that first night—that we would love them when they stopped the beatings—was coming true, and we either didn't want to pay attention to that or else were too glad about today to let it bother us.

We kept on scrubbing and rinsing and soaping up, only avoiding the forbidden area, our genitals. The inability to touch ourselves there—we'd been warned once more as a group by the big man who'd claimed Peter when we'd gotten under the showers not to touch our cocks—only made me more aware of my cock. It seemed so large, so big, as it swung back and forth as I moved under the shower.

It took a while for me to realize that this was the first morning it hadn't been masturbated. I only vaguely wondered if that had been on purpose, if they'd consciously decided not to relieve our sexual tension before this day began.

But if I wasn't tense, I could tell that Andre was after a while. He kept staring over at his young man and seemed to take a small step toward him every so often. Finally, the man said something. "What's wrong, Andre?" They knew our names even if they hadn't been used since we'd arrived.

"Sir, I . . . I'm not circumcised, and you won't let me touch myself and . . .

The three of them broke into loud laughter at Andre's embarrassment. "Bring it over here, Andre," the man said.

Andre was hard by the time he'd walked across the room, and I was shattered to see how utterly vulnerable he was with his erection swinging straight out in front of him. I could feel my own cock rising just because I was hearing such obvious sexual references being made, and I knew I was going to look like that soon—hard and vulnerable at once, my stiff cock once again witness to my inability to deny my sexual truths.

The man reached out and took the soap from Andre. While Red and the burly man continued to enjoy the spectacle, Andre's master lathered up the cock and pulled back the foreskin. He used the washcloth to rub against the flesh, which was so tender that Andre couldn't help grimacing as he was cleaned up. Nor could Andre keep his cock from staying erect. He was being totally humiliated by his erection and by the idea of this man washing his most intimate flesh, and he made no move to object, to rebel, to plead in any way.

"Go on, now, rinse it off," the young man said, giving Andre a playful slap on his ass.

"That's enough. Time for the next stop. Come on out of there," Red eventually said. The three of us moved out of the water and took the towels the men handed us. We left our genitals wet and glistening, not daring to touch them even with the towel, but dried off the rest of our bodies.

The cuffs were returned to our wrists, and we left that building, crossing a small courtyard to another.

"Got three for you, Dan," the burly man said as he directed Peter into the barber chair. "They've been on duty for quite a while, you should have fun with them."

"Punishment?" the older man said as he walked toward the barber chair. He picked up a straight-edged razor and began to sharpen it with a strop.

"No, initiation. But we might change that if this one doesn't keep his legs spread." Peter jerked his thighs apart as soon as he heard that last statement, the first really rough words that had been spoken to us this morning. He'd only assumed a natural manner of sitting, but our carriage wasn't supposed to be natural, at least not when it came to letting our thighs press against each other.

Punishment.

Initiation.

The words played through my mind over and over again,

and I tried to decipher them: That was our initiation. Then were we finished with it? Was this the end of that horrible existence we'd been leading? But there was such a thing as punishment. Did that imply that we could be sent back? Was that the way men who misbehaved were treated here? If it was, I made a silent vow never to give anyone cause to do that to me.

The barber went about his business quickly and efficiently. He shaved Peter's beard and trimmed his hair first.

But that wasn't all. The barber suddenly threw back the chair, leaving the upper parts of it parallel to the floor and lifting Peter's groin up in the air. Without a comment or a hesitation, the barber slapped shaving cream on Peter's huge balls. He grabbed hold of the loose elastic skin and began to scrape away at the sac, just as mine had been shaved at Cantrell's by Peter himself.

The hair had been itchy and annoying when it had grown in on the skin that covered my own testicles during the days we'd first been working outdoors. I didn't look forward to having to have to go through that again. But it dawned on me that they might keep our balls shaved. I might not have to worry about that hair growing back again. Just as the taboo on our touching our cocks made us so much more aware of them, so would keeping the skin of our ball sacs shaven make us more conscious of that part of our body—and a daily fuck would keep us acutely mindful of our assholes.

"Your turn, Tim." Red said when Peter was taken off the chair. It took me until I was sitting down with my legs carefully spread apart as far as I could manage within the limitations of the chair's arms to realize that he had called me by name. They had never done that before—just another indication of how much of all of this was planned. But it was useless knowledge. As the barber spread shaving cream over my face, I knew already that we'd never be able to fight their will just because we understood what it was. The three of us were trapped, and we were the ones who had signed the contract that had sprung the trap on ourselves, after all. So why would we ever fight against it?

Andre was next. When the barber was done, we were all recuffed, and again we were walking across the lawn. This time we were moving even farther away from the hut where we'd slept.

9

The Swimming Hole

They got packs and attached them to our backs. They were heavy, but the straps were well designed, and it wasn't a great strain to carry them. More surprisingly, they also got us sandals, which we could use on our feet.

When Red decided we were all ready and slapped my ass to start us going on our way, there was nothing about it to indicate anything more than a playful camaraderie.

They led us across the grounds. Then we were in a forest on a well-worn path. We walked for miles, it seemed, but the way wasn't difficult, and the sandals were more than sufficient to protect our feet.

Red was by me most of the way, and he usually kept a hand on one of the cheeks of my ass, squeezing it every once in a while. Peter had been wrong. It wasn't the cessation of pain that mattered, it was the presence of appreciation. We wanted to be noted, we wanted our devotion to be acknowledged, no matter how slightly, no matter how intrusively.

I was happy, happier than I had thought possible, especially when he was touching me. He was as handsome as I remembered, with his tanned, lined face, which I decided made him look older than his age. I guessed him for thirty-two or so after I'd had a chance to see him up close for an extended period of time. He seemed nicely built under the walking shorts, boots, and T-shirt that he wore, just as the other two did. He had a mustache whose red hues caught the sun's light where it came through the tree branches that shaded our walkway.

The other two were just as interesting, if not immediately so, since—as my cock was reminding me every once in a while—it was certainly going to be Red who fucked me today, not them.

I wouldn't have been disappointed in them, though. The man with Peter was slightly older than Red and much older than the brown-haired man who took such careful care of Andre. Andre's master was no more than my own twenty-five years, I decided, and perhaps not that old. He had smooth skin, and hardly any hair was visible on his legs, though I supposed it might just seem that way; the sun could have bleached what was there. He seemed even more interested in Andre's body than the other two were in mine or Peter's. He was always making small physical gestures: running his hand up and down the crack of Andre's ass or else resting an arm around his shoulders, just over the top of the pack Andre was carrying.

We finally got to our destination, a small clearing made around a little pond that reminded me of the swimming holes that dotted the mountains back home. The three men went about their own tasks quickly. The packs were removed from our backs. The cuffs were taken off our wrists. Then we were standing there—what did they want from us next? To my surprise, Red and the other two immediately stripped out of their clothes. "Come here," he said to me, "and help me get out of these boots."

He sat down on the grassy ground and lifted up first one foot and then the next. I straddled each of his legs to remove the boot. When I was pulling on the second one, his foot came up and pushed against my naked ass. When the boots were off, I didn't wait for him to say anything but got down on my knees and peeled off his sweaty socks.

He reached up and grabbed hold of my neck. He pulled me down on top of him and wrapped his arms around me. The complete contact of our naked fronts was electric to me. I hadn't had so much touching from anyone since I'd come to the strange estate, and now I was suddenly in a man's embrace.

"You might not have to go back to what you were doing," Red whispered in my ear. "If we tell them the three of you are well trained—that you don't need more of that kind of treatment—you won't have to go back. All you have to do is prove it to me."

Then he rolled over, forcing my body underneath his at the same time. My own arms had reached around his back, and I clung to him, almost desperately. *He could keep me with him; he could decide I wasn't going back to the lawn* . . . .

Then he kissed me. I sucked on his lips until he gave me his tongue. I lifted up my midsection, my open legs went around his, and I kept maneuvering until his hardening cock was poking against my hole.

He drew away, not in quick anger but with slow purpose. He rolled off my body and spread out on the grass beside me, resting on his side and looking over me toward the other two couples. Peter and Andre were just as recklessly working at pleasing their masters. Red smiled when he saw it.

He had a hand on my belly, and he slapped it a little bit. "Go and open the green pack—the one that Andre was carrying. There's wine and a corkscrew in it. Bring a bottle and three glasses to me."

The things he'd asked for were right on top; I had no trouble finding them. I brought them back quickly and held the bottle still between my thighs while I opened it. I followed another order and poured one of the glasses full for him.

"It's good," he announced after he'd tasted it. "Pour some for Brad and Jim." He realized I didn't know the actual names of the other two. "Brad's with Peter; Jim is with Andre." I poured two more glasses and took them over to the men. They had each broken their embraces with the slaves. Brad was lying on the grass with his head on Peter's lap, and Jim was straddling Andre—who was on his back—so that their genitals and hardening cocks were pressed together. They took their wine without saying anything to me.

When I got back to Red, he lifted up his goblet and offered me a drink. Already kneeling, I leaned forward and sipped it.

Red reached over to my exposed balls and ran his hand over their shaved surface. Then he relaxed, sprawling back on the grass. "You know what I've never had? I've never had anyone peel a grape for me. It seems—since you're a slave—you're the proper one to expect to do that for me."

"Are there any?" I asked.

"There's some in one of the other packs," he answered.

I got up and opened both packs, finally finding a bunch of the fruit in the second one. I brought it back and clumsily peeled off the skin from a grape and put it to his lips. He opened his mouth and let it drop in. The sight of his tongue reaching up and capturing it was so erotic, I felt almost dizzy.

I prepared another grape and fed him that one and quickly moved on to get still another ready. I wanted to be busy to cover up my confusion. He was acting as though this was as strange to him as it was to me. He wasn't comfortable with it, or at least he was still only trying it on, making himself used to it.

I dropped more of the grapes in his mouth as I thought. I felt a tinge of disappointment in my new understanding. I played back all the nights I had gone to bed thinking about him and his bright red pubic hair. I recalled all the visions of his thick cock and the memories of his strong arms as he'd fucked me. They had all been important to me during those horrible nights after the lawn.

I was suddenly faced with the prospect that he wasn't the man I'd hoped he was, that he wasn't going to be the practiced master that I'd hoped. I had wanted someone to train me.

I put another grape to Red's lips and thought about all that. "What's on your mind?" he asked when he saw me grinning.

"Nothing, really," I answered. But when I took the next grape and had peeled it, I didn't simply drop it into his waiting mouth. I rubbed it gently up and down his lips, enticing him, I hoped, with the gesture. He let me do it for a while but then moved quickly and captured the grape and my fingers as well, in his mouth. He sucked on them for a moment.

Then he took the rest of the fruit out of my hands and set it aside. He pulled at my sides and drew my body toward him. "Why am I bothering with those," he asked, "when I have these right here?" He sucked in one of my nipples, and I could feel the light touch of his teeth as he nibbled on it.

I bent over his body, resting on my hands on the other side of it to give me a means of staying still so his mouth could work on my nipple. He did it wonderfully, alternating between sharp bites and longer, gentle sucking. He moved back and forth across my chest, taking first one, then the other tit.

By the time he was done, my cock was hard, and there were fluids seeping from its slit. I was caught by a sudden sexual shiver when the still-wet surfaces of my chest first felt the wind against them after he'd left and laid his own head back down on the grass.

"That's a different smile now," he said as he studied me.

I shrugged. "It's just as happy," I answered. I didn't want to tell him what thought had brought on the first—the idea that a slave might train a master just as well as the other way around.

"Are you hoping I'll fuck you?"

"Yes, sir." I leaned over and kissed his heavily haired chest.

"Did you see the condoms and the lubricant in the packs?"

"Yes, sir."

"Get them."

I went into the packs to find what I was supposed to—a jar of grease and a carefully wrapped prophylactic. On the way back I saw that Andre was on his belly, spread out between Jim's legs. He was furiously tonguing Jim's balls. I was surprised by his passion until I realized that there were clamps on Andre's nipples and that the chain that joined them together was in Jim's hand, being pulled whenever he wanted to provoke a more emphatic response from the black slave.

Peter was rubbing Brad's back. The muscular master was on his stomach, with the handsome slave straddling his ass. Peter's hands were working in long, luxurious strokes, smoothing out the hard flesh of the other man.

But I didn't want to be caught watching the others, not when Red was waiting for me himself—I hoped he was doing it anxiously.

His cock was already hard and sticking straight up on his belly as he laid on his back in the grass. There wasn't a smile on his face anymore. For a second I thought he might be angry that I'd taken so long, but I immediately realized that he was only showing how ready he was for this.

He only nodded, and I understood precisely what he wanted me to do. I took the condom and unwrapped it. I stretched the latex along the length of his cock. When it was in place, I took the grease and wiped it over the plastic coating.

I waited for him to move, to let me know how he wanted to take me. But he didn't stir. He finally said, "I think it's only appropriate that you do all the work, don't you?"

I put one leg across his waist and positioned the cock so it aimed at my anus. But I didn't simply force it up my ass. I had waited for weeks for this fuck, so it was going to be good; he was going to remember it so well that he'd be as captured by his desire to repeat it as I had been enslaved by the fantasy of having him return to me all those mornings.

I rubbed the blunt end back and forth against myself. I wouldn't stop the constant, intimate movement until I heard him moan slightly and then lift his hips up toward me. I let his cock slip in, just past the guarding muscles. But when he moved to fuck me more deeply, I moved up, only letting that small part of his erection stay inside my ass. "You wanted me to do the work, remember?" I whispered.

I took his moan for agreement. My legs were splayed far apart now, the knees on either side of his body. I had his cock slide in, past my sphincter. Then I'd force it back out, lifting myself up until I knew that only the fat knob of his erection was inside me. I played with him, keeping the fucking to the least contact as possible, not letting any of the rest of our bodies touch. Only the head of his cock in my ass connected us.

He let me go on that way for minutes. But he couldn't last. I finally took him to the point where he couldn't withhold anything anymore. He grabbed hold of my shoulders and dragged me down and, at the same time, violently pushed up with his hips until he was deeply embedded in me.

He rolled us over until he was on top of me. I was so aware that I wanted this sex to be the best I could give him that I ignored the discomfort. I willed my ass to open as wide as it could, to let him have as much entry as he wanted. I kept my arms around his shoulders and urged him on, even when the hard thrusts were causing agonizing pain as his pelvis crushed against my balls. I never complained, but instead pulled on his body, silently urging him to fuck harder and faster.

He kissed me. Those lips that I'd been feeding with peeled

grapes so he could feel like a master found my own and pressed against them. Our tongues met, and then his pushed deeper into my mouth, as though he wanted to fuck my throat with it even as his cock was fucking my ass.

I forced myself to let the sheathed dick plunge into me over and over again. I refused to resist; I vowed I'd never fight him. I felt our hairy chests as the sweat began to soak them, and I ran my hands over his smooth back and let his muscles ripple under my palm as they powered his hips to continue their thrusts.

When he came, he lifted up his whole upper torso, he threw his head back, and his neck became a hard and clear diagram of tendons and swollen veins. His mouth was open, as though he wanted to scream in victory or agony. Then, all at once, he collapsed, all of his weight pressing on my body. I could feel his chest heave as his breath rushed in and out of his mouth against my face.

We stayed like that for minutes, for as long as we'd actually fucked. I kept my body wrapped around his—my legs and my arms—and I used my hands to lightly massage his head. We simply stayed there, his prick up my ass, slave and master claiming each other.

After a long while, his cock simply slipped out of me. When it did, we both sighed. He got up and pulled the latex from his flaccid penis and smiled down at me. "Good," he said. "As good as I had hoped."

The rest of the day was spent in such a continuing cavalcade of sexual play that I forgot the fear that he somehow wasn't really a master.

We went swimming, and he'd have me dive between his legs, forcing me to stay underwater as long as possible while I sucked on his cock. He had me feed him his entire lunch with my hands and only let me eat from the cloth that he'd had me spread on the grass. There was as much wine as I wanted to drink, but I could get it only from his glass.

I was unbelievably contented during the entire day. I was naked, with a handsome man who was using me for his pleasure. Nearby were two men I knew and liked who were being used the same way, and I could watch them whenever there was a lull in Red's and my activities.

Andre was being subjected to the most constant sexual play. It seemed that Jim's interest in him was as consuming as possible. When Jim wasn't hard and actually fucking Andre or else having the handsome black man suck him, there was a multitude of toys to be applied to his nipples or wrapped around his cock and balls. Jim seemed never to stop being fascinated by the body that was in his control, and he constantly found new ways to position it or cause Andre's big cock to keep its erection.

Peter was less lucky—at least in a way. Brad was clearly very interested in the experienced slave. Peter, I'd noticed, could automatically assume roles that Andre and I hadn't even thought of—graceful bows and fluid little motions of submission came naturally to him. But Brad was not going to be easily satisfied with just those no matter how beautifully Peter performed them.

He put Peter over his lap at one point. The experienced slave knew enough to spread his legs, and as soon as Peter had, Brad began to use his hand to spank Peter's ass. It was no gentle slapping, either, not the kind that Jim and Red did. This one was methodical. It brought bright red and purple colors to Peter's butt as the broad palm kept on striking it over and over again.

Peter fought the desire to resist or escape, but it was obviously hard for him to keep still. He moved his ass constantly, with slight attempts to find a way to make the blows less painful. The sight of his ass muscles clenching and relaxing only drove Brad on. The beating was so relentless and the sound of it was so rhythmic that all four of us eventually moved toward it.

When Red brought me close up, I could see that Peter was crying. There were tears streaming down his cheeks. The image turned Red on. He began to stroke his cock up to a full erection. He put a hand on the back of my neck and pushed me to my knees so that I faced him and his red-colored balls.

He dragged my face in until my nose was pressed against his testicles. I immediately began to tongue them, feeling the soft, wrinkled skin and tasting the salt on it. They were so strange, such an exposed part of an otherwise strong body. It suddenly seemed as if this were some act of ultimate trust that he was performing for me, to let my mouth and my teeth come into contact with his least protected organs. This was a moment when I could have struck back at him. I could have physically harmed him. But I didn't; I made sure my teeth were covered by the layers of my lips and that only my tongue came in contact with his ball sac.

Then he pushed me away, and he did it more savagely than anything he'd done before. He reached over to the pile of things by Jim and Andre's blanket and picked up one of the condoms that was there. He unraveled it over his cock. I stared up at it, knowing it was going to be back inside me soon. He moved down onto his knees and between my legs. He put my thighs around his neck and he pushed into me brutally.

"You should have that—that spanking," he said hoarsely. "I should take you over my knees and let loose against your ass."

"Then do it," I answered, surprised by how immediate and anxious my challenge was.

He pulled out, and his hands roughly turned me over until I was flat on the ground. I bent my legs so that my buttocks would rise in the air, and just as I did, the first blow came.

It was so different from the feel of the lash. It was a hand I knew, one that had been in my mouth, whose fingers had been up my ass. It wasn't some piece of leather being used by a stranger whose face I sometimes hadn't even seen.

The blows came quickly; they seemed to be playing a duet with the sound of the ones that were hitting Peter. I swore to myself that I wouldn't draw away from them and forced my body to keep my ass in the air, letting my hard cock stand at a sharp angle from my belly. My balls began to move back and forth from the force of the slaps.

Then he stopped, and I thought it was over. I pushed up on my arms, getting ready to stand up. I thought he was done. But instead I saw that Andre was being guided over toward me by Jim. The two masters had a plan.

Jim rolled Andre onto his back and told him to slide up underneath me. Jim stopped him just when our mouths were midway on our chests. Then he moved both our heads until we understood that we were supposed to mouth each other's nipples. Andre moaned as soon as my lips went around his; Jim had left them tender from all the play with the clamps. But mine were only barely used by Red's gentle mouth so far. I only felt total pleasure when the warm, wet lips encircled mine.

Jim lifted up Andre's legs, and his latex-sheathed cock moved, hard and ready, toward Andre's ass. I felt a sharp wave of air as Andre hesitated working on my tit only long enough to moan slightly. "Don't you stop sucking him till I tell you to," Jim ordered loudly, and underscored his command with a hard slap to Andre's hips.

The warmth engulfed my other nipple then. Just when it did, I felt the blunt end of Red's cock pressing against me. They were going to fuck us both at the same time. The combination of sensations was awesome. My mind seemed to overload as Red's cock began its pumping again and I had part of Andre's body in my mouth and part of me was being sucked by him.

I could barely find the way to concentrate enough to look up and see Jim's young and smooth body as his well-defined stomach muscles clenched and hardened as he fucked Andre. Jim's light brown hair was hanging down over his head, which was bent to let him watch his own erection sliding in and out of Andre's ass.

Red was going to come soon, much sooner than he had the last time. I could hear that in the intensity of his breathing. I closed my eyes for a minute, forcing myself to focus on the sensation of the fuck, of the hot mouth on my chest. . . .

When I did open my eyes, I saw that Jim was staring at me now. His eyes startled me. They were a darker brown than I'd realized. There was something behind them that frightened me—and made me want him tremendously at the same time.

He reached over and took the nipple that Andre wasn't sucking. He caught it between his fingernails and pinched it hard. It was one more sensation—one too many.

I felt my own cock begin to pump. No one was touching it. It was simply spearing the empty air. But the look on Jim's face and the promise in those eyes and the sharp nails that were digging at my chest along with the incredible feeling of a man's cock in my ass were all too much. A heavy load of fluid shot out of the slit. The waves of it hit against the back of Andre's head. The clenching muscles of my sphincter were too much for the already-close Red, and he came, too, just at the same time, letting me feel his pulsing cock let loose into its latex wrap.

10

History

Red finished attaching the last of the restraints. He reached down and ran a finger over my belly as though he wanted the motion as an excuse to linger just for a few more minutes.

"What do we do tomorrow?" I whispered to him.

His hand didn't stop moving. "You have no right to ask."

The answer seemed so cruel after the day we spent. *You have no right* . . . A single pleasurable day didn't alter that fact.

There was proof in the restraints that held me to the bed, just as they had so many other nights before. He didn't say anymore, but stopped feeling my body and turned and walked out of the small building.

I stretched out, yawning. The day had been wonderful, and not just because it had been different from the others. We'd kept on the sex play for the whole afternoon. My ass felt wonderfully raw from the fuckings Red had given me and from the many times he'd used his fingers to explore my anus. My tits were sore, but not too badly. I was tired, but it was a pleasant fatigue from the activity, the wine and the sun, not the utter exhaustion we'd known after working on the lawns in the sun during all those other days.

"What will happen to us, Peter?" Andre asked now that we were alone again.

"We'll find out in the morning" was the only answer he'd give.

"Do you think they'll take us back out there?" I asked him.

"You sound as though you hope they will."

"I do; I liked it."

"You shouldn't be so quick to think there's no danger in what's going on," Peter said. "You're forgetting something; whatever is happening, it's taking us a step closer to Montclair."

"You know him, Peter, don't you," Andre said. "I could tell at the auction that you recognized him from some place."

"Yes. I knew him . . . in another life."

"Tell us," I asked. "How did you ever get to meet him?"

Peter seemed to hesitate, then he moved around on his cot as though he were trying to become comfortable. He finally began to speak:

"Many years ago, before I even knew that The Network existed, I lived in New York City. I was young, younger than either of you. I had a decent job, but it was something I didn't care about at all, just something to collect a paycheck.

"I even modeled a little bit. But not for the money. I did it because it provided me with the one thing I wanted the most: It made other men want me.

"They'd pay attention to me in the bars, anyhow, but it wasn't enough. I wanted them to lust after me. The first time I overheard two men talking about some fantasy person they'd seen in one of the gay magazines, I realized I wanted to be that person.

"I looked up the photographer and offered to pose for him. I got in front of the camera and did anything he told me to. In a few months the pictures of me naked were in the centerfold. I walked into a bar, and I felt the domination my body and my looks gave me.

"I went out and found other photographers. I'd take

ridiculously small amounts of money if I thought they were good enough to get my picture in print. I became a fantasy symbol, the man they all wanted in the Greenwich Village bars. I'd walk in and I'd know they were whispering about me, talking about some image of me they'd seen recently.

"And I used the power by choosing who I'd sleep with. I went to bed with many, many men. We could do that in those days. I loved the attention they gave me. I wanted it the way other men wanted a drug. I wanted them on their knees, looking up at my chest with my cock down their throat, or I wanted them fucking me, feeling that ass they'd dreamed about. I knew it would be an experience that each one of them would never forget. I was never going to be some trick whose name they couldn't remember. I was going to be a peak experience for each and every one of them. That was the one thing I wanted most in the world—to be noticed and to be remembered.

"The sex got rougher, and I found out I liked it even more. It became more intense, more desperate, in a way. And so was the attention paid to me more intense—and more desperate.

"I discovered something about the games the people played in the leather bars: The one they called the 'bottom' was the one really in control. There were so many other men who were prowling, who were looking for someone—anyone—who would let those games take place, that you were their star if you allowed them their moment.

"I had a list of demands that I insisted on. They had to have the right costumes. If there wasn't enough leather or if it wasn't the right style, then I wouldn't go with them. If they weren't handsome enough in exactly the way I wanted them to be, I waited for someone else to come along who was.

"I'd go through the little motions for them. I'd let them tie me up, wave a leather belt at my ass, make me get on my knees for them—because it was easy. All the time I was laughing at them because they weren't the ones on top. I was. I was the one making the choices, and I was the one who called all the shots.

"There'd be a couple of men who'd lurk in the heaviest of the leather bars who were different. They frightened me. They were the ones whose looks weren't important. Their power came from somewhere else. When I'd play my seduction games with them to see if I could get them to accept my rules, they'd walk away from me.

"I hated them and the disdain they showed me. But I was drawn to them, more and more, every time I would meet one of them."

"And Montclair was one?" Andre asked.

"Yes."

"But that can't be all," I insisted. "I saw the way you two looked at one another. He'd done more with you than just cruise in a bar."

Peter hesitated, as though deciding how much more he was going to tell us. Andre pushed him. "We want to know what this man's like, Peter. Please . . ."

"He was the most impressive of them all; you can imagine that. You've seen him now, and this was over seven years ago. I first noticed him, really, when the other men in the bars would react to him—those who'd gone home with him to an apartment he owned on Fifth Avenue.

"They'd look away when he walked into the bar, as though they didn't want him to catch them staring. And there was this odd mixture of regret and longing on all of their faces. A man would be standing there talking and laughing, and then he'd realize that Montclair had walked in, and he'd become sober and stutter. Often a man like that would have to just leave the place, he'd be so upset.

"I wanted Montclair to want me. His star matched mine in that sex world, the most desired top and the most desired bottom. I threw myself at him. He wouldn't respond. He'd be polite, and he would even buy me a beer or something like that. But he'd never pick up on my signals or give any indication that he was interested.

"One night, after he'd been acting like that for weeks and driving me crazy, I walked right up to him and asked him to fuck me. It was one of the raunchiest bars, one that was on the waterfront over by the Hudson. There weren't many rules in those places back then. I stood in front of him, and I pulled down my pants. I turned sideways so he could see my ass. 'Want it, Montclair?' I asked him. 'It's yours for the night.'

"He looked at me and grinned—just slightly. 'If I took it, I'd want it for longer than one night,' he said.

"'That's all anyone gets,' I told him, 'but they all say it's worth it.'

"'Then, if I only get it for one night, I want it totally.' He put down his drink and walked to the other end of the bar. 'Give it to me right here,' he said loudly. 'And show me how much of it I'm going to get by crawling over to here.'

"He pointed to his booted feet. The other men in the bar waited to see what I'd do. I never even hesitated. I pulled my pants back up and zippered them and belted them up. 'Too bad, Montclair. You go by my rules or not at all.'

"He never expected me to do what he'd told me to do. He knew I wasn't ready. I suppose that was it. He was wise even then. He came back to where I was standing and bought a group of us a round of drinks and didn't mention any of it again until the night was over and he was leaving. 'Someday you are going to crawl for me,' he said.

"He wasn't around much after that. And I didn't pay much attention to what he'd said. I thought it was just bluster, covering up because I'd turned him down in public.

"I just kept on going in the regular ways. They became emptier. There were too many weak men who were playing too many games who weren't interesting enough. I began to think of Montclair more and more, even though I didn't see him. I began to dream about that one night. The feel of the wood on my belly would have been so much more . . . *real* than my evenings in wool-lined restraints. Whatever there was that was on the other end of the floor would have been . . . *better* than the men who'd talk dirty to me but who—I always suspected—would just as soon trade places with me.

"I got into some weird things—making the men who wanted to play top to me buy newer and better leather clothes, as though a bigger and more extravagant costume could make the fantasy they performed bigger and more extravagant as well. It never worked.

"I started to go down—far, far down. I'd drink too much to let my mind flow more freely and not see the shortcomings of my sex partners. I'd go to the backroom bars and do things there where—since there were no real voices or real people—my own imagination could run rampant.

"And all through it, the image of Montclair grew and grew.

"Finally, there was a night when he came back to one of those places. I went up to him. I was drunk. I'm sure my looks were going—bloated by alcohol—but I still had to have looked good, and there were still many men who wanted me.

"But he pushed me away and left the bar. Some guy came up to me and whispered in my ear, 'He doesn't need the showpieces like you anymore; he's found something much better.'

"I was furious. I demanded he tell me what that was supposed to mean. The man started to talk about a strange fraternity where the games became real and the bottoms never thought about their masters' style of dress, where the servitude was absolute and the idea of crawling across a floor wasn't something forbidden and taboo but something the slaves did every day of their lives.

"There was money in it, too. That meant something to

someone like me, at that point in my life where I knew I wasn't doing well with my career—I knew I was fucking it up. I was adrift in sex and work both. Here was a way, he said, for me to go off and have this peak experience with men like Montclair and even come out of it with dollars in my pocket.

"I got a name and address of someone, and I called the next day. I was as anxious as anyone who ever called a priest to ask for salvation.

"I found The Network."

"That's why he recognized you," I said. "What did he say when he made you pull down your shorts at the auction?"

"He told me he wanted to see what all those men in those bars in the old days were after. He wanted to see my cock; since none of them had gotten anything else of value, he told me, my dick must have been awfully big; they had to have been after that.

"And then, after he'd made me pull my pants down, he told me it wasn't that exciting. He didn't have much use for a big cock, anyway. But he did tell me he thought it'd be interesting to see if I'd learned to crawl yet. That's why you two can afford to think of just today and those three men being good to us. But I can't. I'm going to pay for that night in the bar."

"Or else," Andre said softly, "you'll finally be able to do what you know you should have done the first chance you were given."

11

The Salon

There weren't any shocks to wake us the next morning. For the first time in weeks I was able to open my eyes slowly, to let the day begin with that soft focusing of consciousness and not yelling men wielding whips or Red undoing my restraints.

Instead, there was some distant noise. I turned toward the sound and saw the exquisite picture of Jim gently fucking Andre.

Andre's legs were over Jim's shoulders. The young man was softly moving in and out of Andre's ass. The muscles of his hips and flanks were undulating with each thrust. The two of them were kissing, Jim's mouth covering the black slave's with a quiet passion. Andre's wrists were above his head, still attached to the bed, and his light covering of underarm hair was visible. Jim's arms, taut from the strain of holding his upper torso up, looked strong, and their skin was smoothly glossy.

I lay there watching, thinking how beautiful the sight was, being terribly jealous that Andre—and, so far, he alone—could wake up to the feel of such a handsome man's cock up his ass.

Jim's muscles began to tighten, and the tempo of his movements began to increase. I could hear Andre moaning more loudly, as though he could feel Jim's cock swelling that one final time as it approached orgasm. Then there was a short burst of speed in both Jim's actions and Andre's reactions and it was over.

The two of them were coated with new sweat. Jim had collapsed onto Andre's body. But they kept their kiss for a few more beats of time.

Then, still gently, Jim pulled out of Andre, who groaned loudly when the contact was broken. Jim pulled off his condom and tossed it away. He stroked his receding cock once, then moved to undo the wrist restraints.

When he was done with Andre, he looked over and saw that Peter and I were both awake and watching them. He didn't say anything about what we'd just witnessed. He just came to me, and then to Peter, and undid our restraints.

"You can stand up." He went over and pulled on his shorts and shirt and shoes while we got up. Then, still not talking, he came over and pulled our wrists behind our back and secured them with the familiar handcuffs. "Come on, then," he finally said. "Follow me."

We walked over the lawns of the estate. I suddenly understood that we were going to the house itself. I felt the excitement sweep over me as we began to ascend the hill toward it. I'd never even seen it this closely before. Now all the details came into closer focus: how perfectly it was maintained, how thick the vines were that climbed the brick sides, how large the windows were.

Jim led us around to the opposite side of the building, one that we'd never seen before. There was a large swimming pool. Around it was a flagstone patio. Where the patio met the house, there were sets of glassed French doors. We walked up to one of them, and he opened it. He stood aside; we were supposed to enter.

"This is my territory," Jim said. "I rule here. I make all the rules for everyone—except, of course, for Mr. Montclair."

Peter, Andre, and I were sitting on the floor in front of him. We were in the huge room off the patio. "This is one of the special areas of the house, a very special house.

"This is the way it works." He leaned against the wall and crossed his arms over his chest. His legs were muscular and strong looking, with especially meaty calves.

"Mr. Montclair has a very important business enterprise. It's one that calls for the very best minds for analysis and operation. He's carefully recruited his men to be those who'd appreciate his personal proclivities." He smiled when he said the word, finding it amusing.

"Rather than worry about life in the city and be concerned with scandals that his employees might produce if they were left to find their own entertainment, he's brought everyone out here. The employees live in apartments in the house and some of the other buildings. There's everything they might ever want, including you.

"This is called the salon." He waved his hand at the room. "It's dedicated to the pleasure of the people who live on the estate—and to Mr. Montclair's pleasure, of course. You and the others are here, available at all times for all things. I'm here to make sure you're kept occupied and in your place.

"You were introduced to the estate by doing the work that's used as punishment here. I want to warn you that I can send you back out there on a moment's notice and for no better reason than wanting to do it. Mr. Montclair and I did that—sent you to the weeding—because we think that it's only fair that anyone who might be punished understand just what that punishment will be. You know now.

"There are other elements in the routine here that will also help keep your mind focused on your place in this world of ours." Jim reached out and grabbed hold of Andre's hair, pulling his head into his crotch. It was a small but decisive illustration of Jim's point.

"There's a regular regime of exercise that you will perform. It's posted. You'll be observed doing all of the required activities every day or you will be punished." Jim kept on talking, explaining that we were a group of house whores. I was devastated.

"There are no tricks here; don't worry. Nor is there much you'll be surprised by. One or the other of you has already been fucked by nearly every man who works for Mr. Montclair; they've been the ones who took turns waking you in the morning; it's been their way to try you out.

"There are no rules other than those you've come to expect: You're to always have a proper posture, always be willing. The men work indoors, something many of them dislike intensely in many ways. They often come here just to swim or use the gym equipment that's on the other side of the room. A few of them are very . . . imaginative. But most of them are not as . . . exotic as Mr. Montclair or myself.

"It's up to you to entice them, to make yourself exciting enough that sex—something they might not really be after—is something that they take from you. There are lots of props and costumes around. You'll find them. Use them if you have to. If you hold back, you'll find yourself working in the gardens again. Trust me; that's not an idle threat.

"Mr. Montclair doesn't want his employees dissatisfied; he certainly doesn't want any of them to think they have to go somewhere else to find entertainment.

"The room is kept warm at all times; you'll have no need for clothing. There are platforms with carpeting and mattresses all around, in different locations you'll have no problem finding. You won't have to sleep in restraints anymore—so long as I don't find you touching yourself or beating off in your sleep. That's the biggest crime here, that one of you would waste Mr. Montclair's assets for your own pleasure—that's something you sold him with your contract, after all. You'd be stealing if you used it for yourself, wouldn't you?"

He found that humorous and laughed again. "That's all for now. You'll learn your way here soon enough." He stood up, pushing Andre away from him gently. He put a finger under Andre's chin and lifted it up to face him. "You're lucky," he told the handsome black men. "I'm here all the time. My favorites get plenty of attention, and not one of them has ever been known to be bored." He let go of Andre's chin and reached farther down to flick a finger across Andre's chest, pinching his nipple before he walked away.

The three of us stayed together. We didn't talk to the other naked men in the salon. But we did take our lead from them. What Jim had said seemed true: There were no tricks. We found a chart on the wall that laid out the minimal requirements for exercise and chores for each of us. There were over twenty names in all on the sign, something that made me remember the one buyer's remark at the sale that Montclair had an extravagance of slaves.

We saw that the others felt free to move between the salon room and the poolside patio, where they sunbathed on the flagstones—though never on the furniture—and often swam in the pool. Here, in the room, they lounged on the carpeted floor and on the piles of pillows that served as the only informal furniture in the place.

Peter was the bravest of us, and Andre and I followed him out to the pool. Just the idea of diving in was an incredible symbol of freedom after the restraints we'd lived with for so long, we couldn't resist. We fell into the cool water and played around, splashing one another and doing slow, languid laps up and down the length.

After a while, I got out and spread my body on the warm flagstones to let it dry in the sun. I kept feeling my wrists and was still surprised there weren't leather bonds there. I moved my limbs more than I ever would normally just to luxuriate in being able to do it.

Peter got out of the pool and laid down on his side, facing me. His skin was still beaded with water, making it seem even more perfect than usual. His balls were hanging down over his closer thigh. I realized once again how large they were and how elastic the sac that held them was.

He was smiling at me, and I realized why when he gazed at my own cock, which was half-hard. "The idea of being the temple prostitute turns you on?"

"No!" I said it louder than I'd wanted to. "I hate it. It's such a . . ."

"Comedown?" He suggested exactly the word I wanted.

"I thought . . . I thought there'd be more, but I don't know what 'more' would have been like. Was Cantrell's better?"

"Better?" He seemed to have to try out the concept. "Yes, in its way. There was only Cantrell. He kept seven of us in the house. He thought that was the perfect number. Each of us had an assigned evening to spend in his chambers. The sex with him was . . . awesome. I think, sometimes, it was necessary to have so many of us so that each one could spend a week recovering from the ways he used us.

"Cantrell is a true sadist. He loves to inflict pain and to watch men suffer from it. There was a large *X* in his room, at the foot of his bed. He'd have each of us placed in it on our night, and then, after we'd been taken to the limits of our endurance, he'd untie us, spread us on the bed, and fuck us."

"How could you do that? How could you endure knowing that it was going to happen to you every week?"

"It wasn't bad, not at all. In fact, it excited every one of us. He was a real genius at it. It was brutal a lot of the time; God knows, it was. But he was so damned good at it. You felt sometimes like you were the raw material being made into something incredible by a real artist. You have to understand, we each knew that we had an assigned night. That meant that you'd wake up one day and smile because you weren't going to be used that night. You were grateful.

"Then your day would get closer. You'd start to get nervous thinking about it. You'd watch him—Cantrell—and you'd know when he was smiling that he was thinking about just what little devious tortures he was planning for you.

"On the day that you were going to his room, you'd have this stomachache about it all. You'd look at him and have to turn away. Your body prepared itself the whole time, thinking about the night. It was . . . exciting; that's the only way I can describe it.

"And Cantrell knew it, and he was a master at playing with you about it. You'd be doing some little chore—we had those, but there was nothing heavy; nothing like the stuff we had to go through on the lawn happened at Cantrell's house. He'd walk up behind you and tell you to stand up straight. You would; then he'd pull up your shirt and simply stare at your belly, or he'd feel your thighs. Then he'd smile at you and walk away. You could only look at that part of yourself and assume that he'd been making plans for it.

"A sadist like Cantrell isn't going to do the same thing over and over; the belt on your butt or a whip on your back would become too repetitive for him. He'd want you on that *X*, and then he'd go to his implements and find something to use on some totally unexpected part of yourself.

"It went on, forever."

"You had to have hated it!"

"It . . . This world—Cantrell's house or this compound of Montclair's—this world isn't like any other. How you endure, how you enjoy, how you survive, is so different. . . . You'll have to see; you'll have to learn it for yourself.

"I didn't hate it. I was with the six other men. We were proud of it all. We really were. It started out with his masterfulness about so many things. When you first went to his house, Cantrell would say small things to you about yourself and your background. He'd make you want to go through things; he'd make you want to prove something to yourself. He'd find some little element of your psyche, and he'd play it.

"'Oh, you're from the Midwest. No one from there has any backbone,' he'd say; something simple as that. You'd decide you were going to prove him wrong. You weren't going to break down on the *X*, not in a million years.

"And then the group of you would get together, and you'd start this macho thing with one another. You'd tell each other what he'd put you through, and you'd brag about it. It became a strange manhood test, one that was repeated weekly. But the group was there, and you didn't want to give in and let them know that you'd begged him to stop.

"He understood all that. If someone did perform poorly, he wouldn't punish them the way you'd expect. He could use that whip for punishment; don't misunderstand me. He certainly knew how to do that. But when you'd simply let him down by not being a good sexual partner, he'd get you by humiliating you in front of the others. 'Peter doesn't have quite as strong a back as you,' he'd tell one of the other men. 'He broke down much too early in the evening.'

"That was intolerable for him to say that. You felt foolish and inadequate. He was your master, the only one who was supposed to matter in this world, and he was dissatisfied, and he told other people he was. You never wanted to be in that place again.

"This isn't reality the way other people understand it, Tim. This is our own creation, at least partly. We come into it, and we take part in this whole dance with these men and women we sell ourselves to. Things that you talk about that way—things you say you can't stand, that you'd hate—that's not true here. Here you love what you hate in the rest of the world. Here you look for what you avoid outside.

"Besides, there were rewards. Living at Cantrell's was a sexual dream come true. There's only your body. Everything else is taken care of, and you never worry about money, food, a job. The only clothes that you ever got to wear—when you did get them—were ones that made you feel more naked. You had a cock and an asshole and a pair of tits. That was it. That was all of it. And it was more then enough.

"We'd all wait anxiously for guests, too. That was our other great game. Because Cantrell would, of course, provide any people staying over with whatever they wanted. There were so many of them—men and women—that we never knew what would be involved. The guests kept life interesting.

"That and his entertainments. Cantrell understood that we couldn't be kept unsatisfied for an entire week. So he would let the six who weren't to go with him that night have sex with one another. He used to like to watch us, I think, to turn himself on.

"He'd have us play 'games' to decide which three of us were to be on top."

"By winning?" I asked.

Peter laughed out loud, "No, Cantrell was too smart for that. The ones who were to be on top had to be the losers. He had all of us fighting for the bottom, where he knew we all really wanted to be.

"It could be something as simple as a card game or something as vicious as a wrestling match. The three men who lost had to perform stud service on the others. Stephen, the man you met at the sale, and I usually managed to play together so that we could try things with one another. He was the most imaginative of the group."

"Was that why you signed up for another contract?" I asked. "Was it because you found that much in it all?"

"Cantrell was good. He was good enough for me to want more. But he wasn't the best, not at all. The best was the first time I was sold, when I came off the downward spiral I told you about. I wanted this life after that first time. He was the one who really showed me how much it could be.

"I met a man in New York who trained me. That wasn't hot—he was mechanical in his approach—but he gave me enough that he could take me to The Network. He did it only for the money; it was the way he earned his living. You know that the trainers get part of the surplus—the difference between your contract price and what you get at the auction?"

"Yes. I didn't mind that. My trainer gave me so much more than lessons."

"Well, this man does it simply for cash. I could tell that was true when I was with him. There was no passion to it at all. To go through all of that with someone who only thought of you as an exercise . . ."

"But he did get you in," I insisted.

"Yes, yes, there was no problem with that. And I knelt on those same tables you did. They were even in Cantrell's own house that year, too—they change the site often. But that year they were in that same place.

"The man who bought me could barely afford to bid at The Network. He used up all his savings to pay for me." Peter sprawled on his back as he continued his story. His cock began to harden as he brought back his memories.

"We lived out in the country, just the two of us. He was determined to get his money's worth from me. That was clear, and that would have made everything wonderful in itself.

"But he was also determined to make that year the most memorable of both our lives. We explored every fantasy he'd ever had."

"He must have given you that thing you wanted: to be remembered, not to be a simple trick."

"He gave me that, all right," Peter said, smiling. "He certainly gave me that.

"We didn't live very glamorously at all. The really good masters don't need it. I learned that from him.

"I didn't want to go when my time was up. I would have

stayed for the rest of my life, or I thought so then. But he was too smart. He understood all this too well. He knew that once that contract wasn't there to hold me, then our entire relationship would eventually change. Besides, he didn't buy me to love me. He'd bought me to live out his fantasies with my body. If we kept on going, we'd have to know one another even better. I would've ruined things for him.

"He knew we'd slowly evolve into lovers, having quarrels and losing the bonds that the contract gave us. He couldn't stand that, he said, watching the years erode into that boring reality. . . .

"So I went back to The Network, and I found myself with Cantrell and his whips. I was fixated on the money then—my contracts are rich, and the principal is sitting somewhere in a bank gathering up interest. I want to understand more of this. I want to buy someone just like you when I'm done with this contract. Then I can experience it all."

He reached over and pulled at one of my tits. He looked me straight in the eye. "I want to show someone like you everything that my first master taught me. That would make my life complete."

I pulled away from his touch. He laughed at me and said, "You can do that—now, with me—but there might come a day—"

"Why?"

"Because it's never been complete for me. It's still only been my body they bought. Maybe if I owned someone I could find out how it works. If I had a slave, maybe I could figure this out."

12

The Master

"Do you enjoy using my property, Peter?"

We froze when we heard Montclair's voice. Both of us turned and looked up to find him standing near us. He was naked, ready for a swim. "I'd call it impertinent—at least that," he said. But a smile undercut the words' harshness.

I was actually holding my breath as we waited to see if he'd do anything. But he walked by us. He stood at the edge of the large pool. I hadn't seen him undressed before. The front of his body was covered with as much hair on his chest and legs as there was on mine, but the color was darker, actually black, not brown.

His shoulders spread out in a handsome fan of smooth skin. His arms were well developed, with curving biceps and sinewy forearms. His legs were well shaped. Most beautiful of all was his ass, round and so firm; there were indentations on each side.

He flexed, getting ready to dive, and the whole of his body moved in individual parts, changing the visual complexion of his torso, making it still more powerful looking.

His dive was perfect; his arms led the way as he cut through the surface. Only when he was underwater did I dare relax at all. I turned back to look at Peter again. He appeared dazed by the sight of Montclair.

"I'm sorry if that got you into trouble." I said.

Peter only smirked. "There was no question of you getting me into trouble," he said. "I was there the first day I met him."

We watched Montclair swim laps in the pool. He did it with great precision, his arms moving gracefully, mirroring one another's movements. His legs kicked strongly, but with perfect measure, just enough to propel him toward his goal, never more vigorously than necessary.

He kept it up for quite a while, long enough to make it obvious that this swim was a part of his conditioning, not just an idle undertaking. When he finally stopped and climbed up the ladder at the far end, his chest was heaving from the exertion.

Two naked men were there, waiting with an oversized towel. They dried him off efficiently and without his having to say anything. It was obviously part of his ritual.

Montclair walked away from the two men. They looked surprised and not at all pleased. This must have been a break in his routine. He came back over to where we were.

"I'll see you inside, Peter. And you, too, Timothy. Go and find Andre; bring him with you."

He was gone, disappearing into the salon room, before either of us could really react. We jumped up, Peter nearly forgetting and grabbing hold of his swollen cock in an attempt to stop its painful jerking—but he remembered himself. I knew he would keep total obedience with Montclair so close by.

Andre was only off to the side, on the lawn. He was on his knees in front of Jim. The overseer's shorts were pulled down. There was a used condom in Jim's hand, and Andre had his head pressed against his belly.

"What do you two want?" Jim said. His voice made it clear that he didn't like the intrusion.

"Mr. Montclair," I stuttered. "He wants us . . . Andre, too."

Jim reached down to help Andre off his knees. "Go on. When he wants you, you get right to it."

The three of us went to the doors to the salon. Andre and I rushed through them and went up to Montclair. We hadn't even thought of how we should approach him this first time.

Montclair was sitting on a pile of pillows. His arms were resting on one of his knees, which was pulled up. The other leg was stretched straight forward. His cock and balls, all covered with that fine black hair, were resting on one of the pillows.

They were the most beautiful genitals I'd ever seen before. They weren't tremendously large, but they seemed perfectly formed. The cock wasn't circumcised, and the hood of foreskin covered half of the glans. The testicles were held in a sac of lightly haired flesh. The pubic hair that crowned them all was a filled-in arc of black hair against his flat, hard belly.

We waited, not knowing what to expect, but Montclair wasn't even looking at us. I turned back to see what he was staring at. Peter was standing in the doorway. He was frozen, as though petrified by fear. But he was breathing heavily, as heavily as Montclair had been after his exercise.

Rather than hurrying across to Montclair the way that Andre and I had, Peter suddenly dropped to the ground and fell forward onto his front. He used his elbows and his knees for locomotion as he moved across toward Montclair. He wasn't simply moving on all fours, the way we had done so often when we'd first gotten here. He was crawling on his belly. The muscles hardened and relaxed from the strain as he continued to move forward. He kept his legs apart, so far separated that we could see his large balls trailing along behind him. And he was doing it in front of an audience.

Andre looked at me, obviously wondering what we should

do. I simply knelt beside our owner and waited, fascinated, to see what would happen. Andre followed my lead.

Peter finally reached Montclair. He didn't lift his head, but simply moved it until his forehead hit the man's toes. Then he pushed his face even more until his lips were on Montclair's feet, and he kissed them both. He seemed to wait, to see if there'd be any specific order, but there wasn't.

Peter's lips didn't leave Montclair's skin. He moved up the man's calves, onto his thigh. There, as though he had to do something to acknowledge his arrival at the fleshy power of Montclair's upper legs, Peter's tongue slipped past his lips. He used it to leave a slight line of wetness as he made his way toward Montclair's genitals.

Peter's tongue reached the dark folds of the skin that held Montclair's testicles. He stretched the sac out, lifting the two orbs. His eyes were staring up at his master, waiting for some signal—any signal. But there was nothing. Montclair just looked down at the blond man. Peter closed his eyes then. He kept his tongue moving on the master's balls, lifting them up and pressing them against his forehead so he could reach far underneath them for a while. Then he let them fall back down so he could use his tongue to wash the front of them.

Peter's eyes opened up again, and I knew he was beseeching Montclair to order him onto the master's cock, now resting hard and stiff on Montclair's belly. But the man didn't say a word. Peter continued working his extended tongue on the folded skin of the ball sac.

But Montclair was responding. If he wasn't going to admit it to Peter, he showed it to Andre and myself. He reached out and grabbed hold of both of us, drawing us down beside him on the pillows. He guided each of us onto one of his nipples.

I took in the one I'd been directed to, trying to think of every possible thing I could do to make it feel as erotic as I could. My own tongue pressed against the hard, erect point. I grazed it against my teeth, but I didn't dare actually bite it.

I sucked hard. I let it slip out of my mouth once and blew gently on it.

He had a hand on the back of my neck and squeezed occasionally; I could only hope it was a signal of his pleasure. I could see Andre working just as hard as I was on the other half of Montclair's chest. I looked up and saw that Montclair had his head thrown back, as though in a private, quiet ecstasy.

Then it all got to be too much for Montclair. He pushed Andre and me aside and sat up. There were condoms all around the room. He handed me one of the wrapped prophylactics. "Put it on me, Tim."

I was astonished that he was going to let me do that. Even when I realized it was something he was using to humiliate Peter—that he was having me perform this act in order to deny the other slave the pleasure—I felt it was some great privilege.

I carefully opened the outer wrapper. I leaned forward and was able to study Montclair's handsome cock even more closely. There was a faint odor to the secretions that had been caught in his foreskin. He was one of those men who excreted fluids when he was excited. The glans—that part of it that I could see, that part that wasn't covered by the foreskin that still clung to some of it—was glistening with wetness.

The foreskin fascinated me. I wanted to reach down and pull on it with my teeth and fuck the space between it and the cock head with my tongue.

I put the top of the rubber over it. A bit of the moisture stuck to the white plastic. That one space immediately became translucent. The slit was clearly visible. I rolled the edges down, almost feeling sad as each fraction of an inch of his skin was covered. As I got closer to the base, there was more and more hair on the shaft, and I had to be careful not to catch any of it.

Finally, the whole of his cock was wrapped in the white

latex. The glans looked even larger now under the stretch of the plastic. The shaft's veins were even more pronounced, since their bulk pressed against the covering and the purple blood vessels didn't have to compete for attention with the hair or the naturally dark skin.

Through all of it, Peter had kept on tonguing Montclair's balls. When I reached the base, his mouth was right by my fingers, and I could feel the wet spit he'd left on some of Montclair's pubic hair.

I wanted to do more, maybe join Peter by sucking Montclair's cock while Peter continued with the balls. But I understood that I couldn't. I knew perfectly well that Montclair had plans for the other man.

I sat back on my haunches, my legs spread far apart to let my hard cock spear the air. Andre was staring at me and my erection; his own cock was half-hard. Montclair was holding on to Andre's balls; gently, it seemed. The black man's face didn't show any pain or discomfort.

"Let me see how much you really have learned, Peter," Montclair said. He reached down and grabbed his sheathed cock and held it straight in the air. "Suck this."

Peter finally stopped working on Montclair's balls. When he moved back, I could see that his spittle had flowed down onto his chin. He ran his forearm over the bottom of his face to wipe it away. He looked up at Montclair for only a quick moment; then he studied the waiting erection.

He moved forward and let the head of the cock slip into his mouth. "Better than that, Peter," Montclair said. "Show me you mean it."

Peter swallowed the whole length, gagging as its thick shaft entered but refusing to let it slip out. His face turned red from the effort, and tears were forming on the sides of his eyes.

"Look at that, you two. Look how happy he is to have that cock in his mouth after all this time. It could have been there long ago if he'd only admitted that he wanted it."

More tears began to flow from Peter's eyes. "Don't you love it, Peter?" Montclair demanded.

There was no way Peter could talk while that cock was crammed into his mouth, but he forced out a sound that was attempting to voice agreement and seemed to nod his head yes.

"You'd have loved it years ago if you had had the courage to admit it, Peter. It was there for just this if you'd understood what it would mean." Then Montclair took hold of his cock again and dragged it out of Peter's mouth. The blond slave dove to regain it, as though he were frightened that it might have been his fault that it had—or else desperate that he might never get it back again.

"Fuck yourself with it, Peter," Montclair said.

Peter stood up and moved forward until his legs were on either side of Montclair's waist. He was studying the master's face intently now. Peter pulled his buttocks apart in an act that was at one and the same time obscene and beautiful. He lowered the spread ass and moved it back and forth when he had touched the upheld erection. His eyes closed then, as though the physical contact made visual communication unnecessary.

Then, when he must have felt the head of Montclair's cock right at his hole, Peter shoved downward. His face screwed up with pain, but he didn't stop the motion until the entire latex-covered length was buried deep inside him.

Montclair didn't move until that moment. Then he reached forward and took each of Peter's nipples in his hands. He worked them back and forth, up and down, producing a series of pleasurable shudders in Peter's body.

The blond man looked more handsome at that moment than I'd ever seen him. The horizontal muscles in his stomach were strained with exertion as he began to move himself up and down on the master's cock. His chest expanded, and the large pectorals were curving out, making it seem as though he were inviting Montclair's hands to continue their work on his tits.

His haunches were lined with hard muscles that were contracting from the effort to continue to power his movements. His arms went behind his back; even though he hadn't been told to do that, he automatically moved them out of the way. The new posture only accentuated his chest more.

"Doesn't that feel good, Peter?" Montclair said. His voice was turning mean, sarcastic, and bitter. "Isn't that a good cock for you to sit on?"

"Yes, sir."

"I don't know that you've really earned it, though, Peter. Perhaps I should let Andre or Timothy have some of it. Maybe I should push you off and let one of them climb on, let them feel what it's like to have the man who owns you fuck you."

"Please, sir"—Peter's voice was trembling—"don't take it away from me; don't ever take it away from me."

"But you want to be the master—isn't that what you said to Timothy? You can't really want to get fucked by someone else all that badly if you're going to want to turn around and top someone else."

"Sir, if this cock were up my ass, I couldn't even think of anything or anyone else." He meant it. The tears were authentic, and so was the hard cock that was pointing straight out of his belly.

While he kept on moving up and down on Montclair's cock, Peter's own was letting lose a string of viscous liquid that was falling downward. I watched—the way you'd watch a spider's web being made—as it slowly stretched farther and farther until it hit Montclair's pubic hair and became a physical connection between the two men.

Montclair seemed to suddenly twist Peter's nipples harder than he had before. Peter let out a gasp. "Move more quickly," Montclair ordered. The blond slave began to increase the timing of his movements. A red stain began to spread over Montclair's chest, one that was visible even through his body hair. The two men increased their breathing.

Peter's face began to contort—I knew he was getting close to his own orgasm. Montclair bit his lower lip, and his head fell back onto the pillow.

Andre and I watched it all as the pressure and the tension built up and the two men moved quickly toward their orgasms. Just as Montclair began to yell out, Peter's cock began to pump waves of come. The first one struck Montclair on the stomach. Then there was a whole series of smaller, less violent releases that left a trail of his fluids over the master's abdomen.

When the last drop seemed to have left Peter, Montclair shoved up, hard, into Peter's ass. He bellowed now, for his own orgasm had seized every muscle in his body for a single second. And then it was done. The two of them were drenched in sweat. The slave was bent forward, his hands on the sides of the master's chest and his knees pressing against the master's hips.

We all waited to see what Montclair would do, what he would say. The spectacle of it all had been wonderful, more wonderful than I had ever expected.

The master finally used his hands to direct Peter up and off his cock. He only had to nod toward the receding erection to let Peter know he wanted the used condom removed. Peter performed that final submissive act. He was still holding it in his hands, eyeing it as though he were holding some communion cup, when Montclair stood up, his half-hard cock swaying in front of our faces. He looked down at Peter for a moment before he actually spoke: "Tell Jim to send you to my quarters tonight."

And then he left.

13

The Master's Suite

We didn't see either Montclair or Peter for two weeks. Then, one afternoon, Jim came to us while we were sunning by the pool. He was obviously pissed off by something. "Montclair wants you two to go to his apartment. He has some special assignment for you."

"Where? How . . ." Andre asked.

"I'll take you there. Follow me." He turned and began to walk away.

The two of us had to run to catch him just as he was leaving the salon. We followed through the door into the main section of the building. We'd never been in this part of the house. Some of the other slaves came here regularly though. Andre and I had never become friendly with them; we'd stayed together our whole two weeks. They were just as aloof, acting as though they were superior to the rest of us. We had, though, overheard their conversations about their other "duties" and their "special assignments." I looked around, trying to see where those slaves might have gone. I couldn't understand it at first, but the tour we were getting was still amazing.

We walked along a long corridor. After a while, there were open doors on either side of the hallway, and we could look in and see the men—so many we knew—working at their desks and drafting tables. They were all dressed. Their clothes were casual shirts and slacks; they appeared to be just like any other workforce in any other high-tech factory.

We'd never seen them this way. We only saw them naked when they entered the salon. Or else we saw them in the costumes they kept in lockers in the small private rooms off the central area of the slaves' quarters. I saw men whom I was used to seeing in black leather chaps and boots now dressed in polo shirts and khaki pants. There were others who wore military or police uniforms in the salon who were working diligently at their calculators. This was the other side of Montclair's life, the strange business that paid for our fantasies.

None of them paid any attention to us. Two naked men weren't an uncommon sight in the house, evidently. Then I noticed a few men scattered among the others whose appearance was more shocking. They wore no shirts; most had on metal collars. They were at the same kinds of desks as the others, apparently performing the same tasks, but they had on the symbols of slavery.

That answered a question we hadn't been able to answer before. There would occasionally be men who'd come into the salon and into the dark rooms off it who were led there naked and chained by their masters. They would never be allowed to speak to us but would be quickly taken into the chambers. We'd hear the same muffled sounds of their endurance and their sex that we recognized from the times the house slaves were taken into those rooms. But when the men would be brought out, their bodies covered with sweat and their skin showing the hard use they'd been put to, they would leave the salon and reenter the main house.

Now it was obvious that there were employees in Montclair's business who wouldn't have wanted to use the slaves he provided but who had the opposite desires. I wondered how that worked? I remembered now that there were times when Jim and another of the attendants in the salon had been with those men, when they'd been the masters to lead them from the main house into the rooms. Were men like Jim masters hired for their enjoyment, just as we were paid-for slaves? But there were others who were always with the same master, and I suspected now that they were lovers of sorts, men who were equals here in the work space and in their living quarters but for whom a visit to the chambers of the salon was always a possibility.

We left the work area behind and were in what seemed to be public rooms, large spaces with walls of books, so many that they had to be a library. There were billiard tables in one, a bar in that same room. Then there was a dining room set up more like a restaurant, with many different tables.

This, of course, was where those slaves had been taken, to these public rooms, where they were probably the bartenders and waiters, naked men who'd wander through the groups of Montclair's employees, serving them food and drink and their own flesh when it was wanted.

Jim led us up a stairway. At the top, we turned toward the front of the house and finally came to a stop before a large door. Jim knocked. A voice told him to enter. He opened the door, and there, off to the side, was Montclair. He was standing by a desk, leaning over to read something on the screen of one of a bank of computer monitors. He looked up and saw the three of us. "Good," he said to Jim. "Just leave them."

"Yes, sir." Jim stepped aside to let us pass. One of his hands grazed Andre's ass as the black man moved through the doorway, but Andre didn't respond at all. I knew he wouldn't.

The door closed behind us, and then we saw Peter. He was naked, kneeling on the floor. He wore a blindfold. There was a chain across his chest; on each end there was a metal clamp that was attached to one of his nipples. His cock was hard, and along the underside was a line of clothespinlike devices attached to his skin. There was another line of them arcing around his balls.

He was obviously in horrible pain. His body was shuddering from it. He was crying; there was moisture coming out of the bottom of the blindfold. But there was hardly any sound, since there was a gag stuffed into his mouth and held in place by a leather strap that was tied behind his head.

I'd had those things done to me. I knew what torture those innocent-looking clothespins could be. They cut off the circulation in that one area of your flesh, and what seemed to be only a small pinching sensation at first could grow to become excruciating pain. But there was more, there was something worse. When they were left on so long that they created this kind of pain, their removal caused an even more brutal sensation. The blood that'd been kept out of the flesh would rush in too fast, and the feeling was as though your skin had been ripped off.

Montclair knew that. He left us standing there and moved over to Peter. He reached down and took hold of a clamp on the blond man's nipples. He quickly pulled it off. Peter screamed behind his gag. His body lifted up, and he threw his head back in agony.

His blindfold kept him from knowing where Montclair was going to move next. The master moved around, taking off one, then another, clothespin quickly, but never in any order that Peter could have anticipated. First he'd take one from the bottom of Peter's cock, then one from the right side of his balls, then another from that same place; then he removed the other clamp from Peter's nipple.

Montclair moved just fast enough that Peter never gained any kind of control over his reactions. He would howl through his gag in that terrible pain, and then, just before his breathing would be normal, Montclair would remove another.

Peter twisted and turned his body. His legs were shaking

with agony, twitching from the hurt. I could see that he was always on the verge of moving them together to try to protect himself from what Montclair was doing to him, and I could only imagine the self-control that he was exerting to stop.

Then Montclair was finished. Peter's chest was heaving. Montclair was running a hand over Peter's nipples, then over his balls and along the bottom of his cock. The skin there had to be raw; even that light touch had to be more agony. But it had to be less terrible than what had been done to him earlier.

Montclair reached up and undid the blindfold. Peter's eyes blinked madly while they adjusted to the sudden sunlight. He saw us then and was obviously surprised we were there. Montclair removed the gag next, and Peter's tongue hurriedly wet his lips, which had dried out.

"I wanted Peter to show you what progress he made," Montclair said. He had a hand on the back of Peter's neck. "He's a different man than the one you knew a few days ago. Aren't you, Peter?"

Peter didn't answer, but moved his body to put his face against Montclair's hip. He didn't simply rest his head there; he kept rubbing it against the master's slacks.

"But there's more to show you two. Come here." Peter stayed where he was, but only after he leaned forward to keep even the slightest contact with Montclair for as long as he could before the master walked away, out of his reach. Montclair had gone to the side of the huge platform bed that dominated the room. The polished ebony-wood frame was topped with a black leather spread over the mattress. Built onto the main frame were nightstands. He opened one of them and pulled out two of the familiar condoms.

He gestured for us to move closer. We did. He opened one of the packages and rolled the latex over Andre's cock. We were both hard from the excitement of being here, with him, and from having seen Peter's performance. There was no problem keeping an erection right now. As soon as he was done with Andre, he moved and worked on me, mechanically covering my hard cock with the plastic shield. He motioned us back over to where Peter waited on the floor.

Montclair only had to put his hand back on Peter's neck and guide the blond man with the slightest motion to have him take a position on his hands and knees.

That's when I saw the back of Peter's body. There were marks on his ass and his back. They were incredible. Not just because of their strange rainbow of colors but because of their perfect symmetry. They were all at exactly the same angles from Peter's middle, fanning out like feathers that had been drawn on his flesh. He'd been beaten, and he'd been beaten hard, but not in any kind of blind rage. It was obvious that Montclair had actually designed those marks, not simply inflicted them.

"Peter's become very proficient these past few days. I remember when men had to force him to suck a cock or court him before he'd let them fuck his ass. But he's over that now. Peter's attitude is greatly improved."

He put a hand on the small of my back and led me in front of Peter. The hand went to my shoulders, and I knew he wanted me to kneel. When I did, my erection was pointing right at Peter's face.

"Do it," Montclair said.

Peter didn't need any other command. He lunged forward and took my cock. But he wasn't just sucking it. He didn't just put it into his mouth. He swallowed the whole length of it expertly, without any hesitation. I felt the very back of his mouth clamp down on my erection and knew that he had to have been gagging, it was so far back there. But he didn't make any gesture to avoid it or to try to pull back. He moved, but only enough to make sure I was getting the most pleasurable sensations possible.

I was so amazed by having him suck me so powerfully that I didn't watch what else was going on at first. When I did look up, I saw that Montclair was guiding Andre's cock toward Peter's ass. He shoved Andre forward, sending the erection deep into Peter. But the blond man didn't stop sucking me. Even while he groaned at the other intrusion, he kept on moving his head up and down my cock.

Montclair stood back. "Faster, both of you. Fuck him. Fuck his face. Fuck his ass. Faster!" He reached back down and slapped Andre's ass hard. My black friend was shoving his cock in and out of Peter as hard as he could now. Each thrust produced a loud smack as his flesh hit Peter's buttocks.

Montclair was moving toward me. I knew he was going to hit me. I tried to hold him off by taking control of the blow job I was getting and shoving my cock ever deeper down Peter's throat. Now he did gag, and his face turned an angry red. Montclair didn't care if the veins in Peter's neck were engorged by the effort he was making; he slammed me across the ass, and I shoved myself so far down Peter's throat that my pubic hair meshed against his lips.

Montclair's hand struck me again, then again. The sting on my ass was sharp, and the sound of the beating seemed to echo in the room, making it seem even louder than it would have in the carpet-covered salon.

"Now, Tim, now." Montclair said. As if the bastard even controlled my orgasm, I shot. At that same moment, Andre started to groan loudly, and I could see the by-now-familiar signs of his coming as well.

We both slumped over Peter's body afterward, drained by the sex. Our cocks were still inside the other man. Montclair hadn't given us permission to take them out, and we knew better than to try that without his sanction.

Montclair was kneeling now. His hands were running over Peter's body. The master was smiling, obviously pleased with his favorite's performance. "Isn't he becoming something very remarkable?" I didn't believe he wanted us to answer. I didn't speak. I just saw the expression on his face.

There was something in it that I'd never seen before. Perhaps I had. Perhaps I'd seen a glimpse of it that day we'd been taken to the swimming hole or a few of the times that Jim had been looking at Andre when they'd first had sex. It was certainly affectionate. But it wasn't just the affection of an adult loving another. It had more to do with how a master reacted to someone he'd actually trained, to some personality he'd had a hand in creating.

There was something else to it as well. It had something to do with ownership. I know that. It wasn't a lover looking at his beloved. But it was someone looking at something he owned, which he did, most certainly, and cared for a great deal.

Whatever it was, Peter adored it. He kept my cock in his mouth, but now his tongue moved against the wrinkled plastic that clung to my retreating erection, as though he wanted to touch me and thank me for what he was receiving if he couldn't do it to Montclair.

"Back out of him," Montclair said. As soon as my cock was freed, Peter turned and ran his tongue over Montclair's thighs while the master removed first mine and then Andre's condoms and tossed them away. "Take them, Peter, and get them ready for this evening."

Montclair simply stood up, only taking a moment to fondly run a hand through Peter's sweaty hair, and then he walked back to his desk. He sat down with obvious confidence that his order was going to be followed.

Peter watched every motion and didn't move himself until Montclair had begun reading. It was only then that Peter seemed to be willing to give up the hope that his master would return.

He stood up, slowly and obviously in pain from the position he must have been in. He nodded to us and began to move stiffly toward a door at the other end of the room.

The next room was obviously for servants. In the center was a very plain platform bed, almost as large as the one in the other room. Peter fell onto it with a loud groan as soon as he'd closed the door. Andre and I both just stared at him, once again looking at the pattern the whip had made on the back of his body. I could see now that it was repeated on his legs as well; his thighs and his calves had that same fan of welts.

It took Peter a minute before he could painfully turn himself over and look at us. He ran a hand over his chest and down his belly, where it rested. He smiled. "I keep forgetting that I tried to get him to fuck me on my own terms." He found that funny and laughed a bit. "You, my friends, are looking at a very reformed bottom."

Once he spoke, all the reserve Andre and I'd both felt was gone. We got on the bed and moved up to lie down beside him. He put his arms around our shoulders and gathered us to him. I'd forgotten how much larger than us he was. He seemed strangely like some older brother. He must have felt the same fraternal emotion because as soon as we were next to him, he kissed us each on the forehead.

"I need some time to pull myself together after that," he said. We didn't doubt it and didn't speak, just stayed there beside him. Andre moved his hand down to Peter's belly and then onto his cock and finally cupped his big balls. He massaged the sore skin gently, coaxing a sigh from the blond man. "Don't do that," Peter said, "That belongs to Montclair." Andre took his hand away and let it rest on Peter's thigh instead.

I leaned down and took one of his nipples in my mouth and tongued it softly, getting still another sigh from Peter. I remembered doing this back at Cantrell's. I was sure the tit was harder, longer, more scarred now. But Peter obviously didn't want me to stop. I felt his hand as it went to the back of my neck and pushed down a little, just enough to encourage me to continue what I was doing.

After a few minutes, he pulled us both away from him and sat up. He moved backward to rest against the wall. We sat up ourselves, cross-legged on the mattress.

"Well?" Peter said, "welcome to my world." He thought it was funny and laughed. He pulled on my neck again and dragged me to him so he could kiss me. "Nice cock, Tim. Just the right size to make sure I feel it. I never did get a chance to suck on it before."

"You don't like mine?" Andre joked.

"I'm just glad each of you was doing what you were doing. From the feel of that thing of yours up my ass, Andre, I think I probably would have choked to death if it'd been down my belly."

"Thanks a lot," I said.

"I'm getting good at it, aren't I?" Peter said, forgetting the jokes. "I damn well better be."

"What do you mean?" Andre asked. "What's he been doing to you?"

"Doing to me? He's been showing me just the kind of enthusiasm he expects me to have. He brings in other men and kneels beside me while I suck them, slapping me around if he thinks I'm being hesitant about anything to do with sex. He . . .

"Look, none of that makes any difference. Because none of that's what he's really been doing." Peter shrugged. The movement must have caused some of his muscles to hurt, because a quick wave of pain swept over his face.

"I've spent the past couple of weeks performing like I never thought I could. I've gotten to know that man's body better than I've ever known any other's. I've washed it in his bath, I've been fucked by it, I've sucked every part of it. I've eaten off his belly; I've slept underneath it with his cock up my ass.

"I have never, ever, been the center of one man's attention to this extent in my life. Never. I'm exhausted, I'm euphoric. I'm in shock, I'm in pain, I'm . . ."

"You're in love?" Andre asked.

"You know, even if this stops right now, even if nothing else happens, I will remember these two weeks for the rest of my life."

"More than you do that first master?" I questioned.

"Even more than that," Peter responded

"And now he owns your cock," Andre whispered.

"He owns yours, too," Peter answered.

"Not this way," Andre said, "not the way you meant it when you told me not to touch it. That was different. That wasn't for a fee or for a contract; you meant it."

Peter closed his eyes, but not to express any kind of anger or hurt. It was more as though he wanted to block out anything but the pleasurable dreams he was having, as though even the reality of looking at the room or at us would have diluted something precious.

"When it's all done—the work, the torture, the humiliation, whatever *it* has been—he always takes me in his arms. It's like a reward, some prize I get that's more valuable than any other. Sometimes, as big as I am, he'll just sit me on his lap. Other times, he lies beside me on the bed or sits beside me on a couch. And he kisses me, and his hands, which might have just been tormenting me or torturing me, start to caress me while his tongue moves inside my mouth.

"When he does that, he takes my cock in his hand, and all he has to do is massage it or simply hold it and I know that—without any dramatics—he's claiming it. He usually masturbates me, and when I come, it's the most powerful thing in the world. Once, when he had me tied up, with my arms over my head, he knelt down himself and sucked me off. Sometimes he fucks me, but more gently than usual, jerking me off while he does it.

"I live for those moments, those touches. It seems as though I could only lessen them if I let someone else touch me. That, or I'd make the sensation of coming with him less intense. I don't want those things to happen. I want it to be like this forever."

"How is it different that first time?" I asked. He'd already made that original master of his sound so complete that I couldn't imagine anything more.

"My first master was a physical genius. He wanted to explore everything, the way I told you, and just being the one who shared all that with him made some kind of bond between us. But Montclair has reached into my mind, into something I suppose I'd call my soul. He's taken everything physical I could imagine and added to it some other dimension. I can't explain it more. With my first master I felt uniquely appreciated. With Montclair I feel . . . loved, I suppose."

Then Peter opened his eyes. "And you two? How has it been for you?"

Andre scowled. "House pets, that's all we are. I get a daily fucking from Jim that he's trying to turn into the plot for a romance novel."

"Andre's not exactly having a magical time of it, Peter," I teased. "He's much in demand . . ."

"For the most boring sex I've ever thought of. Jim likes to think I'm his in some way. But that emotion—his own version of love—means that every time has to be softer and more gentle. He lets the other men know that he doesn't appreciate their taking me, not that it matters much."

"There are these rooms all around the salon," I started to explain. "You weren't there long enough to see them. Some are lined with leather and have big mirrors and a whole lot of sex toys. Others are supposed to be re-creations of locker rooms or toilets . . ."

"Like a well-designed bathhouse used to be," Andre said.

"And we're just there to be taken to the rooms. The guys get dressed up in clothes they keep back there, and some of them—only a few—get into wild scenes."

"It's their fantasy we're supposed to fulfill," Andre admitted. "That's why we're there. And some of the men are heavy. Unfortunately, it seems most of them have favorites, and we're not often the ones they choose. But it is, really, like living in a bathhouse in the old times. The only difference is we have no say now about who takes us to those rooms.

"We end up having sex ten, twelve, times a day. Then we work out—swim, sun ourselves, that's about it. It's so boring compared to what you're talking about."

"Boring?" Peter smiled at that. "I doubt there are many people in the world who'd consider sex twelve times a day boring."

"It was great at first," Andre admitted. "It seemed just wonderful to have to do nothing but have sex all day. But there's no buildup to it; there's no tension, no pressure. It wouldn't even bother me if some of the men want to be bottoms. That'd be fine. That's the master's choice; he can write the script. But there isn't that . . . stomachache of anticipation. There isn't one—at least not yet—who makes you stay awake at night and wonder what he'll do to you the next morning. There's no one who demands so much you think you can't do it."

"Yes. I understand all that." Peter drew Andre to him and embraced him. "I understand what you want, how far you want to be taken." We sat there silently for a short while. "I think you're probably going to get a taste of it tonight."

Andre sat up and looked at Peter. "Is Montclair going to use us?"

"Not him, not tonight. But he has guests coming, and you two are the entertainment. I convinced him to let you do it even though there are others who are usually given this chance. That's what he meant about getting you ready. That's what we have to do now."

14

The Dinner Party

I stood against the wall, staring across the room to where Andre was in the same position as I. Our legs were spread apart, our arms behind our backs. We were waiting for the men who were in the next room, having drinks before their dinner.

The small pieces of clothing Andre and I were wearing were the most forceful proof of that first lesson Peter had given me when I'd been at Cantrell's: that clothes could make us feel more naked than we would if we wore nothing.

There were strings around our waists that held up a small pouch made of incredibly soft black leather. The bottom of the pouch was attached to another string that went up through the cracks of our asses to the waistband. The constant feel of that piece of thread against my anus was one of the most subtlety erotic sensations I'd ever had. Even the slightest shift in my body made it move against my asshole and made my cock stiffen.

There were armbands around each of our biceps that were made of the same soft leather, another one around our foreheads, and then other bands around our ankles. The pieces of skin seemed to make the rest of our bodies more noticeable than they would have been. The leather was so supple that you could see every bulge of our cocks and balls through it.

The pouches weren't tight at all; that would have defeated the purpose by pressing our genitals up against our bodies and making their outline less obvious. The pockets of leather were loose enough so that our penises and our testicles could move easily within them.

The sound of men's voices seemed to become suddenly louder. Andre and I tried to look to see them come through the doorway into the dining room. We both seemed to realize we were breaking a rule and were back to facing one another just in time, just when they entered. They took our presence for granted. "Montclair, your house is just as amazing as we were told it would be." The man who was talking was the first one who came into my field of vision. He spoke with a slight accent I couldn't identify. He took a chair with his back to Andre. He was older than Montclair, or most of the other men in the house I'd met so far, probably about fifty. He looked very fit, with a ruddy complexion that suggested outdoor sports. He was wearing a suit, but his jacket was open, and even through his clothing I could see that he was well built. His chest was barrel-shaped and his waistline was slim.

"I enjoy many of the finer things, Harold. I'm only happy to have learned that you share some of my particular appreciations."

Montclair had gone to the head of the table and was also sitting down. Just as he did, Peter walked by me and toward the other end of the room, where there was a door leading to the kitchen. It was our signal to move with him.

Andre and I both went through the swinging doors together. The cook and his helpers paid no attention to our near nakedness. They must have been used to this. The appetizers—perfect bits of pâté with small triangles of toasted breads and dollops of condiments—were waiting for us. We each took a set of the plates and started back to the dining room.

". . . I wasn't sure how my particular form of enterprise would work in the international trade," I heard Montclair say when I'd come back through the doors. "There are certainly going to be many people who'd be offended. I simply never expose these activities to them. We meet only when it's absolutely necessary, and then in the city, not here."

I suppose I had simply assumed that the man I'd serve would be the same age as the one Montclair had called Harold. But he was much younger, no more than thirty. I reached over and put the plates in front of him. He paid no attention to me at all, but began to eat. I was so surprised by the youth, the huge size, and the attractiveness he showed when I was close to him that I nearly shook.

The man was blond and clean-shaven. He had thick, curly yellow hair that was a contrast to his skin, which was as deeply tanned as Harold's. He moved easily, fluidly. If I knew that Harold was well built for his age, I could also tell that this man was extremely well developed. His biceps were so large that the suit he was wearing had to have been specially designed for him.

He had sharp blue eyes. He smiled well, meaning it and enjoying whatever it was that was giving him so much pleasure.

I went back to my position against the wall. Andre was already in place. Peter had already opened the wine for the first course. He poured for Montclair to taste and then, after the master had given his approval, filled all the men's glasses.

"I'm glad that our friends in Paris made this connection for us, Montclair," Harold said. "It can make so many things so much easier. We import a great deal of the electronic hardware in Europe, and we would be most interested in taking on what you manufacture. I'm sure you'll find that Olaf can handle your marketing very well. After all, I've trained him myself."

Montclair smiled in a way I'd never quite seen before. It had some air of conspiracy about it. "I've heard that the training was quite . . . complete."

All three men laughed then. They all were done eating their first course, and Peter was again taking the lead and motioning for us to clear their plates. We cleared them and brought their soup course from the kitchen.

"It's not really that unusual," the one named Olaf was saying. "I know you've met our friend Hua from Hong Kong. He regularly takes slaves from his harem and trains them to work in his business."

"Hua is a very peculiar case," Montclair responded. "I'm sure there's nothing equivalent to this, even in his history. You were, after all, purchased at a sale and went through a contract, one very much like our Network's. Now you're done with the contract and have become a full partner in the business."

"You don't have it quite right, Montclair," Harold said. He was smiling at Olaf. I could place their accent now; it was from somewhere in Scandinavia. "Olaf still has a contract."

They'd picked up their spoons and begun eating. Montclair was looking at Olaf with a different expression now. There was, unmistakably, a hint of lust in it. I could understand that. The three of us who were standing there, always available to him, were all good-looking. But Olaf was exceptional in every way.

"How can that work?" Montclair said. I admired the way he asked his question casually, between tastes of his soup, not hinting that he might actually be very interested in all this. I'm sure he was.

"You know that I was purchased on the block," Olaf said. He spoke so nonchalantly about that, making it sound so inconsequential that he'd once been a commodity in a slave auction. "It was in Paris. I'm Swedish, you know, not Norwegian like Harold.

"You're right; it's something very much like your Network that we both belonged to. Ours is perhaps more brutal than yours, actually. There are parts of it that can't sustain the examinations your Network can allow."

"How do you mean that?" Montclair asked.

"There are many more dubious contracts in the European system than there appear to be here in the United States. For instance, there were Arabs in the sale with me who couldn't speak any European language. I can't believe they entered into the pact with full knowledge and permission. And there's the length of some of their contracts."

"Many of them are sold for life," Harold explained.

"That would excite a great number of people I know." Montclair said, looking at Peter, who was filling the wineglasses. Peter's face became deeply flushed.

"Perhaps," Olaf admitted, "but I'm one of those who wants to hold out for the choice. I find it more . . . dynamic."

"Perhaps that's only because you came to this as a slave," Montclair suggested.

"I doubt that. I've been so completely involved in both roles. I'm sure I can speak from a well-rounded point of view."

"You're confusing me even more," Montclair said. "You came to Harold via the auction in Paris, and you say you have a contract between you, but now you describe yourself as a master."

"I learned a great deal from Harold. You see, Mr. Montclair, our sexual contract was something that made us both extremely happy. I was young, only eighteen, when I began it. Harold was more than my master, he became my mentor and my father. He insisted, when I asked for a second term in his service, that I attend university as a part of it. Then he began to take me into his business as well.

"Over those years—with the freedom he gave me himself, not by using any tricks—I was able to explore my sexuality completely. I had a lover, in the usual sense of the term, for most of my university career, in fact. He thought that Harold was a relative of some sort. I would disappear for whatever periods Harold wanted me, and because it appeared to be a family matter and something that involved a very rich relative, my lover never objected. I was able to find out what that kind of relationship was like. I enjoyed it and him. I still see him occasionally, and he's never understood exactly what goes on in the rest of my life—what it was that meant we couldn't maintain our relationship.

"I also played with a number of leather men. I had to travel a great deal once I began working for Harold's firm. I was in Germany, Great Britain, the Netherlands, and so on quite often. I would always go to the bars or meet people through mutual acquaintances. Harold had insisted that I develop my body to his liking. I'd already been athletic and active, but with the training he demanded, you can see that I've become quite large. The men I'd meet could only see this Nordic master in front of them.

"I began to take to the role and discovered that this was really what I wanted, what I wanted to be. I owe Harold much. I have never regretted my time in his service and never will. I enjoyed loving that other man as an equal. There was a soft gentleness to it that I find appealing. But the most exciting thing of all, for me, was to be a master."

"You didn't mind this change?" Montclair asked Harold.

"No. Not at all. I adored watching the way my charge was developing. It would have been easy—if I had wanted it—to force him to stay within the tight confines of his slavery. He had, after all, signed that right over to me twice, at the sale and when he wished to have his contract extended the first time. But the sexual evolution of another human being fascinates me, especially when I can enforce the right to watch it closely."

Their soup was done, and in the middle of this amazing

story we had to move and clear the table again. There was another course waiting in the kitchen. I had to remind myself to slow down, that we were supposed to be doing this at a certain measured pace. I wanted to get back as quickly as I could.

". . . I bought Olaf his first slave when he was twenty-two." That's what I heard as soon as I came back into the dining room. "He was very good with the man, a bit too harsh, perhaps, but he had him very well trained in a short time."

"He's just gone." Olaf said, and I could hear a sense of loss in his voice. "I would have liked him to sign another contract with me. He was too frightened that he might never escape it all if he did. He didn't want to leave this life, though, and he went back to the Parisian auction. He knew perfectly well that I could attend that sale and reclaim him. But he begged me not to, to let him go on with his fantasies and not force him to merge them as much with life as I insisted."

"I've always been told," Montclair said as he began to eat the newly delivered food, "that former slaves are the most harsh masters."

"I'm sure we are, Mr. Montclair." Olaf replied. "We know so many secrets."

"You seem to be keeping one from me now," Montclair said as a new bottle of wine was offered to him to taste. "You still haven't explained this private contract between the two of you."

"I have every intention of allowing Olaf to become my heir to our business," Harold said. He watched, smiling, while Peter poured him a new glass of wine. "But I believe the younger generation should earn their place in the world. There is a certain amount of stock that goes to Olaf for each year that he fulfills a certain private agreement with me."

"Harold has a certain number of days which he can

claim." Olaf was more willing to explain details of the contract. "I, to keep our pact, must be ready to submit whenever he claims them."

"So you live your life as a master, with your own slaves and life, but Harold can alter that at his own whim?"

"Yes. Precisely." Olaf said.

"You're able to have a complete life, then, having both sides of your nature fulfilled."

"No. There is no longer a part of me that desires to be a slave, Mr. Montclair. I will do that for no other man but Harold."

"What a terrible shame." Montclair studied the huge Swede; his wineglass was in his hand. He sipped from it, but I could see that his eyes never left Olaf. "I would have enjoyed discovering many things about you."

"I'm afraid, Mr. Montclair, that you'll only discover how good I am at marketing." Olaf was perfectly able to keep up the banter that Montclair was throwing at him.

Montclair took a new route: "Of course, Harold, you could do a new business partner a great favor and use some of your special time to show me this fascinating side of Olaf's personality."

"No, no, Montclair. As much as I would enjoy doing that for your sake, I have only a limited number of days, and I must make them count. Not for me, you understand, but for Olaf. I discovered very early on that my young friend enjoys the public displays of his slavery a bit too much. They let him escape from what's happening and allow him this idea that it's theater, something performed for the audience as much as for the master. I can't allow him to have that diversion if he's going to really be with me."

Montclair looked at Olaf. I could imagine his mind moving with ideas of what he would like to do with the Swedish man.

Peter silently motioned for us to clear the last of the dinner. When I reached over to retrieve Olaf's plate, one of his huge hand's grazed my naked hip. I thought, at first, it was a mistake. But then he squeezed it sharply, as though he wanted to test how firm it was.

The three men had left the dining room when we returned. Peter carried a coffeepot, and all three of us had a cup and saucer, for our masters. They were in the living area, and we went there to serve them.

Peter went about the room, pouring while Andre and I got them each a glass of cognac, as we'd been instructed. We delivered all of the beverages and then took a place behind the masters. Once again, I was staring at Olaf.

The small pouch was getting uncomfortable again. All through the meal I knew that each of the three of us had suffered from our cocks hardening and softening. The other men had to have seen that—the leather didn't hide a thing—but no one had said a word about it. Now, standing even closer to Olaf than I had before, my cock was getting more erect than it had so far this evening. It pulled the string of my small piece of clothing more tautly against my asshole. I felt the rubbing, and it only made things worse, made my cock get harder.

Trying to take my mind off of him, I looked over at Peter. But he was in at least as desperate a situation as I. He was looking intently at Montclair, and the head of his cock was slipping over the top of his small piece of clothing, its red knob engorged with his desire to be closer to his master.

At that moment, as though he knew what Peter must have been thinking, Montclair snapped his fingers and pointed to the floor in front of him. Peter jumped to fall on his knees between Montclair's legs. He put his head on Montclair's lap and stayed, quietly, in that position.

"You gentlemen," Montclair said to his guests, "are of course welcome to have the other two in any way you'd like."

"I'm sure we'll take advantage of your offer," Harold said.

"There are more, you know, in the other part of the house . . ."

"Knowing Olaf's tastes as well as my own," Harold answered, "I'm sure that we're going to be quite happy with what you offer us here.

"I have an appreciation for dark-skinned men myself," Harold went on to explain as he turned to look at Andre, who was staring back at him. "This is one of the most handsome I've seen in some time. Such perfect flesh." He reached toward Andre, who understood Harold wanted him to move closer. Andre did, and the older man's hand was quickly wandering up and over Andre's hips and buttocks.

Harold moved Andre to have him stand by his chair so that he could continue the exploration, which was very quickly producing a thick erection in Andre's pouch. "Olaf, on the other hand," the older man said as he reached up to fondle Andre's hard flesh as it was trying to fight its way past the leather barrier, "is quite happy with the type this other one is."

It seemed so strange, even now, to have someone verbalize my appearance in such a cool, calculating fashion. But my discomfort didn't keep me from seeing the hand that was pointing to the floor beside the chair in front of me. I went and knelt beside Olaf. He rested his elbow on the shoulder closer to him. That was all he did to acknowledge my being there. It seemed to take my breath away, that he would both want me and yet take me so much for granted.

"You're planning on being here for at least a week for these business discussions," Montclair said. "Of course, you can keep these two if you want for that period. If you tire of them, just let me know. I'll find adequate substitutes."

In the whole time I'd been at Montclair's, I'd never heard such an ominous threat. I looked over at Montclair and remembered when I'd first seen him at Cantrell's. There'd been a feeling then that he was going to be my master. The intuition had been overpowering. But I'd misread it. He would buy me; that was correct. But he wasn't to be the man I'd been longing for.

I looked at Peter, and I saw just how completely he'd been fulfilled. His quest had ended. He'd submitted to Montclair unconditionally. Peter was changed; he'd subsumed himself into Montclair. His peace was in giving up the war he'd fought against himself.

I wasn't looking for that peace. I was looking for my wizard, a master who'd transform my life into something spectacular even if he and I were the only ones who understood that it was happening.

I hoped I'd found that man here, that he was the one with his arm on my shoulder. This huge Scandinavian was going to bewitch me. I knew it. I also knew that just as I'd learned to offer myself to the people who inspected me at the auction, I would have to learn to offer myself up to this man. Whatever else, I could never let him be so dissatisfied that he'd need another of Montclair's slaves. He had his own, right here beside him, and I would have to be the one to prove it to him.

15

Olaf

I stood watching in amazement as Olaf struggled to press the barbell. He was on his back, on a weight-lifting bench, wearing only a jockstrap. He began every morning this way, working on his body with a great passion that he said fueled him for the rest of the day.

He'd already gone through a series of warm-up exercises before he'd moved onto the weights. I was sticky with drying sweat all over my body. Dressed only in a jock, just as he was, I had been made to go through the first part of his routine with him. My muscles ached from the exertion; they hadn't been worked like this since I'd been on the lawn when I first arrived at Montclair's.

I was standing at the head of the bench, between two vertical poles attached to the top of the bench, as Olaf continued to force the weights up, then to slowly let them fall downward, stopping them just before they touched his massive chest. His face was contorted with the strain of lifting the barbell. His stomach was tightened so much by the labor that I could see the hard muscles etched out in horizontal lines across it.

I looked down and saw how close the elastic pouch of my jock was to his face. I always stood in this place; I was supposed to be ready to catch the weights if his grip failed.

But he wouldn't have anything to do with my cock and balls no matter how close to his face they were. Not in the morning. I tried to forget about them and instead just watched his body. I hadn't gotten over my awe of it. It was probably the most intensely muscled torso I'd ever seen. His arms were most impressive, especially as they burst with the exertion of lifting the weights. I'd never before been with a man whose triceps and forearms were so perfectly developed. My old habits of judging a male's arms only by the size of his biceps was long gone.

Finally, with one last, loud groan, he forced the bar up as far as he could and let it slip backward onto the slots on the poles, where it could rest. As soon as he'd put them back there, Olaf let out a huge noise, and his arms dropped to his side. He rested there for only a moment while he recaptured his breath.

When he stood up, he reached over and picked up a pair of dumbbells. There was another pair for me. I tried to hide my dread of them as I picked them up. We stood there in our jocks, facing one another, and began the whole series of exercises that he insisted we perform every morning.

By the time we were finished, there was a fresh coating of sweat on my skin. I was even more sore than I'd been after the first day. I hadn't thought that would be possible, but I'd forgotten how painful it can be to work on muscles that were only beginning to get used to exercise. I was sore on top of my soreness.

I'd once just said that I couldn't go any further, that I'd done all I could do. Olaf hadn't answered. I was crying; I just didn't think I could lift the dumbbells again. He stood behind me and had begun to whip my exposed ass so hard with a strap that I'd yelled for mercy, but he hadn't given it to me until I'd picked up the weights again. He'd made me start all over that morning and go through the entire routine from the beginning.

I hadn't made the mistake of letting my arms say they were too tired to go on again.

Finally, we were done. As he did every morning, Olaf collapsed into the easy chair in the corner of the room. I didn't need to be told what to do now. I immediately went to my knees and buried my face in the sweaty jock. I felt his big hand on my neck. "You learn so well," he said softly while his hand kneaded my flesh. "So very well." He spoke the phrase as though it were a lullaby.

I took in the smell of his damn jock. He insisted on a new, clean one every morning. And every morning I could get the odor of him fresh from his workout. It was something he demanded, this learning to love his smell. As he'd taught me to, I tongued the elastic fabric every once in a while, making sure I was tasting him as well as smelling him. There was the expected saltiness there, but since the sweat was so new, there was sweetness also.

My knees were far apart, my hands were behind my back, my mouth was open. Those were his constant orders for me. I could feel him getting hard under the jock. I tried to encourage the erection, following its growing length with my tongue and my nose and attempting to move the loose foreskin under the elastic. If I could get him hard enough quickly . . .

He stood up, his movement forcing me to lean far back. The awkward position of my arms kept me from gaining any balance, and I fell onto the floor. He simply stepped over me.

I jumped up and followed him into the bathroom. He stood in the middle of the tiled room and waited for me to get back on my knees. I grabbed the waistband of his supporter with my teeth and pulled it downward. I kept the jock in my mouth all the time it took me to drag it over his thick thighs and past his knees. Only when my forehead was flat against the floor would he lift up his feet and step out.

I took the jock and stood up. I walked back into his bedroom. Beside his bed was a futon he'd had brought in for me the first night, telling me I was going to sleep there as long as I was with him. I opened my mouth then and let the damp jock drop down on top of a pile of his other used supporters and briefs. He'd said I wasn't to have another pillow. I was to sleep with his underwear in my face. He'd beat me, he warned, if he ever woke up and discovered my face anywhere else. I wasn't to touch the garments with my hands, either. I could only use my mouth to carry them and, as I did now, to arrange them. There was one pair of the very skimpy European-style briefs with a larger piss stain than the others. Its smell was stronger. I always wanted that one on top, where I could push my nose against it.

When it was done, I returned to the bathroom, where Olaf was waiting. I turned on the faucet. When I had the temperature exactly as he'd taught me, he stepped in.

I could take off my own jock and follow him then. I took the soap and a washcloth, got back on my knees, and began to lather up his feet. He'd help only a little bit, lifting up first one foot, then the other, so each could be washed. Then he stood there while I began to wash his legs. I started on his calves. He'd been teaching me the names of the individual muscles. I couldn't remember them all the time. These, on his calves, were especially hard. It was something that he was very proud of. Definition of that part of a body was terribly difficult, and even competitive bodybuilders weren't always able to develop their calves as well as he had.

I moved up onto his knees. Then I could start on the hard chunks of his thighs. I rubbed them carefully with the cloth. There was only a little stubble here. I moved around to get the back. When I'd gotten to his buttocks I was able to move over the two rounded mounds and even wipe the cloth in the cleft between them. He'd taught me to pull the buttocks apart in order to clean his asshole. I did it, as always, amazed at the sight of his hole.

He didn't like me to be lazy during his showers, though. As much as I might be getting a thrill out of seeing and touching his anus, that wasn't the purpose. I moved to the front of his body again. His cock was hard. I soaped up the cloth and ran it up and down the hard length. Then I washed his balls. They were like mine, not as large as you might think with a cock as big as his. But I loved the sight of them. I then reached up and washed the hard span of his abdomen.

I had to stand for the rest. I ran the cloth over the huge chest. There was noticeable stubble there. He remained motionless while I cleaned off his forearms and then the big biceps and triceps and the other arm muscles that were so exaggerated after the recent workout.

He automatically lifted up so I could clean his armpits. The small growth of hair there was the most pronounced on his body. Did I dare say anything? I moved around to the back and ran the cloth over his huge shoulders. I kissed the side of his neck; the water was running down all the time, soaking my face. But I whispered into his ear, "I think it might be time to shave your body again, sir."

He didn't get angry. He only ran a hand over his chest and then under his arms. "Yes, after you're finished."

I put down the soap and then got shampoo. There was a ledge built into the shower. Olaf sat down and allowed me to pour some of the lotion onto his hair. I massaged it up to a full lather. Then he stood and rinsed off.

I quickly washed myself. Then I turned off the water and stepped out of the stall. He was waiting. I usually toweled him dry at this point, but he obviously wouldn't want that this time.

I got out the shaving mug and ran hot water from the tap. I took the brush and used it to heat up a heavy lather. I took the brush and, again kneeling, soaped up his calves and thighs. I had gotten a safety razor—he didn't yet trust me with a straight edge—and, with excruciating fear and care, began to scrape off the stubble.

I'd so often thought of shaving a body as being some kind of ultimate humiliation. I could think of it only as something that a master would do to his slave. But Olaf—as he did in so many ways—had turned my mind around. He was fanatic about his bodybuilding. It wasn't a simple case of narcissism, but he had to be able to study the minute changes in his torso as he worked on it. What would have been a heavy growth of body hair had to be removed so he could see himself.

I'd done this only once, that first morning I'd spent with him. It had been a long process, one that had to be done slowly. He'd warned me that I'd suffer just as much if I missed any of the growth as I would if I cut him. I wanted to do neither. But it wasn't just that I was avoiding punishment. I didn't want to be responsible for marring anything on a body I'd just discovered the night before to be as close to perfect as any I'd ever been close to.

Now, a week later, I loved it more and was impressed by it more than ever. When I'd finished with his legs, I lathered up the front of his thighs and his balls. I was afraid I might move too quickly over the top of his legs in my desire to get to his testicles and had to consciously slow myself down. I shaved the big masses and then found myself holding on to the small, silk-skinned sac. I ran the blade over it, not just carefully, reverently. There was a triangle of pubic hair standing on top of his crotch, but that wasn't work for the blade. I did have one more thing to do here, the most exciting part of all, one I wished I could save for last but knew I couldn't.

There were some hairs that grew along the base of his cock. It was hard from all the attention I was giving his body. I had to fight the urge to suck on it, but I'd painfully learned to wait for a command from him to do that. Still, because of the duty I was performing, I could grab it and hold it steady with one hand while the safety razor glided over his erection.

I stood up again. I wasn't allowed to shave his ass crack; that wouldn't be seen and so wasn't a concern. Now I soaped up his belly and his chest. Here the skin was so taut and the muscles were so smooth that I could make long runs with the razor, scraping off large expanses in single strokes. He was watching me, his cook still hard.

I moved around to his back again. He'd taught me before to shape his hairline on his neck with the blade. That's what I did next. There was also a minute amount of hair on the small of his back. Even though there was no real justification for shaving that now—very little had grown back there—I did it just to be thorough.

When I was done, there was only one other part of his body left for me to worry about. He lifted up his arms again, and I shaved underneath them.

"Good," he pronounced. "Not one cut."

I didn't answer. How could I? What would I have said? Good thing, or else I'd have been beaten. He efficiently shaved his own face then, the one part of this ritual he kept for himself. When he was done, I waited—with one of the thick towels—and wiped him dry.

I went and got the scissors from the bathroom cabinet next. I took them and trimmed his pubic hair. As I said, it wasn't to be shaved, but kept as close-cropped as it could be with the shears.

As soon as I was done, he left me. I finished drying my own body. Then I hung up the towel and went about the next task. As I'd shaved him, I'd been rinsing off the razor in a small bowl on the floor, not in the sink. I opened the safety razor now and cleaned it out, carefully retaining the small bits of hair that had been caught inside and those that were still on the blade itself. I used a hand broom to collect the other hairs that'd fallen on the floor.

When I was sure there weren't any stray hairs, I took a superfine mesh strainer that Olaf had brought with him. I poured the bowl of water with the shavings over the strainer. Today's remains were meager compared to the much larger accumulation on the first day, when he'd just gotten here to Montclair's house and hadn't been able to really take the time to care for his body while he'd been traveling and staying in hotels with Harold.

I put the mesh strainer over in a corner, letting it rest on the rim of a wastebasket. When the hair had dried out, it'd be collected and put with those other hairs from his body. He was collecting them for me, he'd said. If we were together long enough, I could eventually have a pillow made of them, and it could replace, or complement, the pile of underwear I used now.

Olaf was sprawled on his chair, wearing a robe. It was collected around his waist with a cloth belt, but it'd separated even with that tied about him. I could see his now soft cock and his balls easily. He was reading some report. I went to the door and found the expected tray waiting there. It was delivered every morning from the kitchen. I brought it in.

I didn't say anything as I carried it over to him and set it up nearby. I poured him coffee first, serving it black, the way he liked it. There was juice and a glass of milk as well. There were various rolls, and I buttered them for him, leaving the plate of them within easy reach. I took the newspapers that were also on the tray and opened them and spread them on the arm of his chair.

Then I got on my knees and snaked my head up beneath his robe. There was a sharp taste of soap on his balls. I didn't let that stop me from running my tongue all over the smooth surface of his sac. He liked my mouth on his testicles in the morning, just like this. I'd stay here, the way I had every day we'd awakened together, while he ate and read. It could only be for thirty minutes, it could take a couple hours, so long that my legs and my back would cramp and the posture would be nearly unbearable. But he wanted my tongue wet and hot against him while he went through the rest of his morning routine. It was an important part of learning, he'd told me, something he knew that every slave must do with a new master.

The new hairlessness of his skin was exciting, just as it had been that first day. It seemed as though his flesh were much cooler this way. I kept my mouth on his balls and felt his cock rising, pressing against my forehead as it got harder from my ministrations. And just as he told me I would learn to do, I was beginning once more to contemplate being his slave.

The most wonderful symbol of all this was that tiny, growing pile of body hair in the bathroom. "A pillow from your master to you," he'd said. God, I wanted it to be that. I honestly did. It seemed terrible now to think that he'd be leaving so soon, that I'd never have a chance to have that gift from him.

"You must assume that every master you're with is the master for the rest of your life. A master is not some trick from a bar. You must give him everything. Who knows," he'd said that first night, "perhaps I'll buy you from Montclair and take you back to Norway to live with Harold and me. If I decide to do that and you haven't resigned yourself to me, think how much more difficult you'll make it for yourself."

It'd seemed like a heavy threat when he'd first spoken to me that way. But now it was different; it was like some forbidden fantasy. It wouldn't come true. He was leaving soon. Their business with Montclair was nearly done. I'd go back to the salon again and back to that emptiness. After this week with Olaf, it would be unbearable.

He lifted up one of his legs and rested it on my shoulder, pressing me closer into his crotch. My forehead was rubbing against the roughness of his trimmed pubic hair now, and my nose was pressing against his hardening cock. The weight of his thigh on my back was heavy but warm; the big muscles rested quietly on my body. I could barely hear the pages of his newspaper as he turned them above me.

I could never know what determined his erections. There were times when I'd work as hard as I could to get him excited while I was there, underneath his robe, and it would do no good. Other times, he'd get hard quickly, as though something amazingly pornographic were going through his mind. I did know that my own cock was almost always erect. I couldn't forget it; it was so hard that I was usually in pain. There'd be a long string of precome hanging off the tip of it when I stood up and a stain on the floor where a puddle had gathered.

I don't know how long he kept me in that position that morning. It might have been an hour; it could have been more or less. It didn't matter. When he reached down and pushed me away, I still wanted to stay in the heat between his legs where he'd begun sweating so deliciously. When he was freshly shaved, there was nothing to soak up his body moisture. There was stronger flavor to it then, even more musky than it had been earlier.

He got up and went to the closet. I was expected to take care of his most intimate needs in the toilet, washing him in the shower, shaving his body. I was expected to sleep with my face in his worn underwear. But it wasn't necessary for me to be involved with his outerwear. He'd choose and put on his slacks and his shirt himself. But his going to the closet was a signal for something else.

I got up and went to the dresser. I got a pair of his briefs and a pair of his socks. All the socks were the same black color and fabric; all of his underwear was the same style and the same white. I could handle these now. They hadn't touched his body yet; it was only after they had that my mouth would have to be used to take them off him. I was waiting for him when he came over to the bed with his other clothes, which he draped over the covers. He stood there and lifted up a foot so I could slip the briefs up onto his ankle. Then we went through the same thing with the other leg. I pulled up his underwear onto his waist.

I'd been taught to reach down and adjust his genitals so they rested comfortably. I did it now, feeling a bit of wetness on the head of his cock. I tried to get my hand out of his briefs without wiping that moisture off. I managed to do it and then secretly smeared the precome on my cheek so I could feel it dry.

I knelt back down and put on his socks for him. He always wore black loafers during the day. I'd polished them last night, careful to make sure they shined when I was done. I went to the closet and got them for him. He was already buckling his belt by the time I returned. I put them on the floor in front of him, and he stepped into the shoes.

He never wore an undershirt, and he never used deodorant. There was often a ripe enough smell in his shirts at the and of the day that I could have just as well used them for a pillow as the other things. But he'd only had me rub my face in the shirts a few times when he wanted to play with me. He was buttoning up the shirt he'd wear today when I stood up.

"I will be a while. I'll see you at lunch. Spend your time reading the papers. I'll quiz you this afternoon.

"I'm ready now," he ended. It was another signal I'd been taught. I went over to where the underwear was piled up on the head of the futon. Beside it was a length of black leather. I brought it over to him.

He took it and then wrapped it around my neck. "Why am I doing this?" he asked. It was simple rhetoric, something we went through every morning.

I answered, "So I'll remember I'm a slave."

"Whose collar is it?"

"Yours, sir."

"What does it mean that you wear my collar?"

"That I'm your slave, sir."

"Will you forget that while I'm gone?"

"Not while I wear your collar, sir."

He stood there for a moment. This wasn't so usual. I felt his hand on my head. "You give me great pleasure." It was one of the kindest things he'd ever said to me. Before I could decide if I was supposed to respond, he left.

16

The Sacrifice

The sound of the door opening woke me up. I bolted onto my feet.

"Lazy today, Timothy?" Olaf never used the short form of my name.

"Sorry, sir." I was lucky; there wasn't anything that was out of place, I'd done the reading he'd told me to, and the room was cleaned in the way he'd ordered it done every day.

He walked over to his chair, the one I'd come to think of as his throne. He was carrying my lunch in a porcelain bowl, the same way he had every day I'd been with him. I went over to him and knelt between his legs. He reached into the bowl and brought out a piece of cut broccoli. He got the selection of raw vegetables and fruit—the same thing we'd eaten on the lawn—from the kitchen. It "amused" him, he said, to feed me himself.

I was starved. I'd only had what had been left on his tray for breakfast. It was another of his amusements, to have me eat his leftovers. It helped me, he'd said, to learn to pay attention to all of his activities, something that was "becoming" in a slave.

I took some slices of cucumber from him next. He was studying me intently; he always did. I'd never had myself under such scrutiny before. He'd even come into the bathroom and watch me on the toilet sometimes, as though he wanted to see even that part of my bodily functions up close.

The cherry tomatoes he put in my mouth next were richly ripe and fresh from the garden. They had much more flavor than ones from a market.

"I'm very horny this afternoon, Timothy."

I didn't dare say anything.

"I spent the morning thinking about fucking you." Olaf put a wedge of sweet pepper in my mouth. "But now I see your beautiful mouth so closely, and I'm wondering about using that instead." I ran my tongue over my lips. "What do you think I should do, Timothy?"

"Whatever you like, sir."

"Now, Timothy. I've told you many times before that isn't a very good answer for a slave. Remember, I've been where you are. I understand so much more about it than most masters do. It's always so much more interesting if you think about your master's pleasure. What would I get if I chose to fuck you?"

I looked at the bulge in his crotch and knew he was already getting hard. I moved my eyes up to his. He was having fun with me now. I could see it in his expression.

"If you want to fuck me, sir, you can see if I've learned the lessons you've taught me on how to clench my ass muscles to make it more pleasurable for you and on pushing up and down with your thrusts so you get as deep inside me as possible."

"Of course, if I were to fuck you, I'd take the time to beat your ass as well, wouldn't I?"

"Yes, sir, to warm it, to make me more aware of it." That, I knew, was what he wanted to hear from me.

"What could happen if I chose to use your mouth instead?"

"You could see if I'm any better at controlling my gagging,

sir. You could give me that lesson in it that you've told me you think I need." He'd said that after the last time I'd sucked him off, when he'd made me burn with shame because, he said, my technique was so amateurish.

"But if I used your mouth, Timothy"—he ran a finger over my lower lip—"I'd lose the pleasure of slapping your fine, hair-covered butt. I couldn't see the way the skin took on the rosy color I like so much."

He took his hand away from my mouth and went back to the bowl. He began to bring out pieces of fruit now, a dessert, he'd call it.

"There's no reason you can't still do that, sir." It seemed as though the skin on my buttocks was suddenly twice as sensitive. When Olaf used his hand on my rear, the sting would last for hours afterward, he was so strong. He always left me in humiliated tears after one of those sessions. It was part of his training, though, that he insisted I continue to ask him for more. He thought it was an important part of a slave's place that I should always remind him how much I enjoyed whatever attention he gave me.

"I do want your mouth, but I think it will excite me less than if I beat you and fucked you. Haven't you some suggestions on how you could make your mouth more stimulating?"

"You've already said feeding me was making my lips more attractive, sir. Perhaps if I used them on other parts of you now . . ."

"Yes, you could do that."

"I could suck on your nipples, sir, and show you how much I'm trying to learn to please you."

Olaf put aside the bowl and smirked. "Do it, Timothy."

He leaned back in his chair and waited. I'd been through this before; I knew what he wanted. I lifted up, not standing but halfway there. My teeth went to the top button, and I began to undo his shirt. He loved having me do things this way—the carrying of his jockstraps and underwear, undressing him. . . .

The buttons were awkward to unfasten. I'd learned that I couldn't stop just with the first few. I had to finish the entire line of them. I finally reached his belt. I used my teeth to pull the shirttails out from under it. There was only one button left. Only then was I allowed to go back up to his chest and spread the halves of the shirt apart and reveal the huge, shaven chest.

He hadn't moved a bit during the whole of it. He simply watched me go about the labor, occasionally glancing down to make sure my cock was still hard. It was so hard, it ached.

I moved to the right nipple. There was a hole in the flesh where Harold had pierced him. The hole was used, I'd learned, whenever Harold took advantage of his contract and claimed Olaf. There were other piercings in his body—his other nipple, at the head of his cock, on the bottom of his ball sac—where rings would be inserted by his sometime master. I ran my tongue over the tit, feeling the empty space and wondering just how much it had hurt to have that done and what it must feel like when the rings were put in there.

I suddenly had an image of myself with those piercings. I imagined myself watching Olaf attach rings to my body. The vision was so intense that my cock actually jumped, as though it might come by itself, without any more provocation than that visualization.

Olaf sighed. I looked up, never taking my mouth off his nipple, and saw that he'd thrown his head back against the chair. I could feel the hard cock still caught in his pants as it pressed against my naked belly.

I trailed my tongue across his smooth chest to the other nipple. As soon as I got there. I put a hand on the first tit, gently pressing on it in the exact way he'd taught me he liked.

The sigh repeated itself. Then his hand was on the back of my neck, resting there.

I spent about fifteen minutes moving back and forth across his chest, sucking on one tit, then nibbling on the other, finally repeating every move on both of them over and over. The sounds from Olaf increased as the pleasure continued, and his cock was ramrod hard now. I could feel the outline of its erection even through the pants.

"Enough, Timothy, enough of that." There was an urgent sound in his voice.

He pushed me away, back down onto the floor on my haunches. He reached into the back of his pants and brought out a wrapped condom. His eyes gestured toward his crotch, telling me what to do next.

I had to struggle to unbuckle the belt. It was always the most difficult part of undressing him. But I accomplished it more quickly than I'd ever been able to before. I undid the snap at the top of the zipper and then pulled the metal down over the lines of clasps until I could see the top of his small white briefs. I had to pull harder to get the zipper over the mound of his erection.

Then I took the waistband of the shorts in my mouth and tugged at them, forcing the elastic band over his engorged cock. He didn't move to help me, and it was even more difficult than usual to get the elastic down, underneath his balls. But he'd never have let me stop until both his cock and testicles were exposed; it was one of his encyclopedia of rules.

Finally, it was all done. Then he handed me the condom. I unwrapped it. I took the rolled-up white plastic and put it at the top of his thick, uncircumcised cock. I rolled it down over the bulb at its head and over the white length of its shaft.

"Now, Timothy," he said very softly.

I dove on his cock, leaning my head as far forward as I could so the angle was as good for him as I could make it. I swallowed down the whole of the thing, forcing myself not to cough and sputter against the intrusion into my throat. His hand was on the back of my neck again, but it wasn't guiding me or cajoling me on or anything like that. It was just resting there, as though this were only what was expected of me.

It was, after all, just that: what was expected of me. I was to have my mouth and my hands and my ass ready for him at all times. If I hesitated, if I showed anything less than complete enthusiasm . . .

It just isn't enough to say that he'd beat me if I were guilty of those things. A beating meant so little; it was just a form of entertainment for him. He'd used his palm and his belt and various leather implements on my body often. I'd already translated their sting into a special kind of kiss between us. I often spent the day thinking about him and wondering—not at all unpleasantly, never in the sense of worrying—whether he'd do that to me when he came back to the room.

I wasn't afraid of his beating. I was afraid of his displeasure. I'd never had this kind of master before, one who understood what he called "the secrets" of being a slave. No one had ever made me feel so handsome and so desirable; no one had ever made me wonder what would come next, not with dread but with anticipation.

I'd spent these days in the room with him desperate to please him and knowing all the time that there were at least a dozen other men in the salon who could be called up at any moment to take my place, sending me back to that room where I'd just be another in a crowd of naked and almost indistinguishable bodies for the bored workers to use for easy sex. I didn't want that to happen. I wanted to stay here with him, with this salty smell of his shaved crotch in my head and the sweat of his body on my skin.

He began to thrust, the sure sign that he was going to

come. I moved even more quickly up and down his cock. The latex was warm now; I was so used to its faintly intrusive taste that it nearly disappeared from my consciousness, and I was able to imagine my tongue actually moving along the thick purple veins of his cock and feeling the smooth skin there.

His hand grabbed the back of my head much more forcefully now. He shoved my head forward, and I began to gag even more. My hands went to his hips; they involuntarily were going to push back, to try to let me escape from the trap that was threatening my breath. I willed them not to. I willed myself to stay there. I could feel my head beginning to become light from the lack of oxygen. I was suffocating on his cock. Then, with a loud roar, he came. His hands let go of me all at once. I could move backward. Just as I did, my tongue could feel the pulses of come beat against the latex. One, then another, then another; a seemingly endless flow of him pushed against the plastic and drained downward, back toward his stomach.

He gently pulled on my hair, urging me back, off of him. I didn't want to give up yet. His cock was still hard, and I could have gotten so much pleasure from holding it quietly inside me. But I knew better than to fight the obvious order.

I stayed there on my haunches, studying his cock, still wrapped in its protective sheath. I could see the liquid as it gathered in the pool at the head now. I could see his testicles relax after the orgasm, pulling down on the sac. His hand left its grip on my hair and moved to rest on my right cheek. He just held it there for a moment.

"Please, sir . . ."

"Yes?" he asked.

"May I please come?"

"Have you earned it?"

"Sir, it hurts so much. You didn't let me come this morning. I've been hard almost the whole time since you left, just thinking of the shower and shaving you, and I couldn't get my mind off you and your body."

"Have you earned it?" he repeated.

"I . . . hope so," I said, never sure what the answers were to questions like this.

Then there was a knock on the door.

Olaf had no care for privacy; I'd learned that. He called out to tell whoever was there to enter. I recognized Harold's voice. "A very handsome picture indeed."

The door shut behind him. "I take it we're interrupting something." I could see that Andre was with him.

"Just Timothy begging to have an orgasm. He's a terribly greedy young man." I could tell from his tone of voice that Olaf was teasing me now.

"Perhaps you should let him," Harold said.

"I think it's time for him to get me and my guest a glass of wine, a much more productive enterprise for him, wouldn't you agree?"

I stood up immediately and went to the bar. They had all seen me walk around with a stiff erection many times. I was losing my embarrassment about it more and more every day.

I brought the glasses back. I handed one to my master and then the other to his business partner. I caught Andre's eyes, and we exchanged quick, silent greetings.

"Your slave could actually perform a service for me which would allow him to have his orgasm at the same time," Harold said.

"What?"

"Andre is still not reacting as well as I should like to many things. I've had him once already this morning, but he could do with another lesson in getting fucked."

"Put me away, Timothy," Olaf said. That was the signal to pull up his briefs and rezipper his pants and buckle his belt again. It was all the same exercise as before, but more difficult and time consuming. The two Scandinavians were used to this going on while they carried out their business. They didn't mention my activity at all while I struggled with my mouth to fasten Olaf's slacks.

"I suppose I could allow it," Olaf said, "if it's a question of doing you a favor."

They waited until I was finished. Then Olaf took out another condom and rolled it over my cock. There were containers of oil around the room, carefully placed so he wouldn't have to get up and move when he wanted to fuck me. He reached for one now and greased up the plastic coating. "You're getting a treat, Timothy. Have you ever fucked Andre?"

"No, sir."

"Have you wanted to?"

I smiled now. "Yes, sir."

"Do you think Andre wanted this?" He tugged at my hard cock.

"I don't think he's going to get any choice in the matter, sir."

"Of course not. But do you think he'll enjoy it?"

"I'll try and make him, sir." The whole thing—doing this as a favor for my master's friend and getting to fuck Andre's hard, coffee-colored ass—was exciting enough. But I knew I was going to be doing it in front of Olaf. I felt as though I were going to perform some new and secret act for him.

"Now, Timothy, ask Harold just exactly how he would like it done."

The older man didn't wait for me to go through any formalities. "Just take him, Timothy. Fuck him gently. I only want him even more accustomed to it. You two are friends; I understand that. There are many ways to get fucked. Andre should learn them all. Be kind. It will be a pleasure to watch you both act in that brotherly way."

Andre moved to join me. We were on a small rug between

the two masters. He must have received very specific instructions on how to do this from Harold, since he immediately got on his back and spread his legs apart and bent them up at the knees. I could see the deep cleft between his buttocks. His eyes were dancing, as though we were getting to do something that we'd always wanted to but simply had never had the chance to do.

I moved in between his thighs and felt my hard, greased cock slip over his testicles and then onto his belly, where it laid next to his own larger one. I dropped down on top of him, and when my lips reached his, he was ready. We kissed. He moved his ass then and wrapped his legs around my waist. I was forced to move my own hips until the head of my cock was rubbing in between his cheeks. There was one spot where there was more warmth, a slight bulge in his flesh, a hint of an opening, and I knew I'd very easily found his hole.

He'd actually done it himself, just maneuvering our bodies until I was instantly being invited to fuck him. I couldn't have performed that so well and was both pleased and jealous at the same time. I thrust forward and felt my cock slide into his body. We both opened our mouths, and I could feel more than hear his slight moan escaping.

I began to fuck him with a steady rhythm, one that he met and accompanied me with. We rolled onto our sides, our bodies resting on one of his thighs, both of us keeping up the movement.

I was so excited from having sucked Olaf and from finally having Andre that I didn't think I could hold back much longer, certainly not while he continued to entice me. This, I knew, was just what Olaf wanted me to learn how to do, this constant clenching and unclenching of the sphincter muscles and the gentle, urging movements of his hips.

It was simply too incredible a sensation to resist. I started to move more quickly as I felt my orgasm coming so strongly that I knew I couldn't fight it off. But besides the physical excitement there was the knowledge they were watching. Our masters were sipping wine, studying us. Andre began to breathe faster as well; his hands gripped my shoulders harder, urging me on. I came so hard, I thought I might lose all control. It seemed as though my body had endless fluids to release; endless amounts of come had to he emptying into the latex.

When we were done, we stayed in our embrace on the floor. Andre finally pulled back just enough to look at me more intently, still smiling. He leaned back over and kissed me gently on the lips.

"You can see, Olaf, why I enjoy this young man so much," Harold said.

"I can, certainly."

"You'll understand, then."

"Understand?"

"I have asked Montclair for the two of them. I was going to give you Timothy as a present as well as keep Andre for myself. They are compatible, very attractive together. There'd be no problem with both of them in our house in Oslo."

"Yes?"

"I offered him a great deal of money. I felt they'd be worth it. He accepted the cash offer."

Andre and I were staring at one another. He nodded his head; he knew about all of this. But there was a hesitation; there was something else involved.

"There is another condition to the sale, Olaf. Montclair won't give it up."

Andre and I were still attached, my cock still inside him. We hadn't been given permission to break our embrace. But we could both look over toward the two men from where we were. They were still on their chairs, holding wineglasses.

Harold reached into his shirt pocket at that very moment. He brought out something that I couldn't see. He handed it to Olaf.

"Now?" Whatever it was, Olaf was shocked; it was the first time I'd ever heard him talk that way, so uncontrolled.

"Montclair insists on a weekend of your service if he's to agree to release the two youths to us."

"You can't do this!" Olaf was angry, furious.

"I have the right to hand you your rings whenever I please. You have no right to refuse them. Take off your clothes."

"Not for Montclair!"

Harold moved quickly; he slapped Olaf square across the face. The imprint of Harold's hand was a bright red on Olaf's cheek. "For whomever I choose," Harold said, his voice low, almost growling. "I have the complete right to your body for whatever I choose. I have the right to make my claims on you for whatever reason, at whatever time. It was what you promised. It is our contract."

My cock was hardening inside Andre. The idea of my two masters together, one of them serving the other, was electric. Andre could feel my reaction. His hands ran over my shoulders now, just slightly caressing me. We were watching a scene play out in front of us, one even more dramatic than our fantasies.

"But for Montclair . . ." Olaf spoke more quietly now. "You know, Harold, that his motives are so low; simply to want a man because he was told he couldn't have him is so unimaginative."

"It is simply the price of having Andre." Harold moved over to us. He put a hand on Andre's head. "When you are my slave, Olaf," he said, not looking at my master, "you are simply one of them. My favorite, usually, and you know that, but no more. You are now something of value that I have with which I can purchase something else of value.

"Montclair's request seems like a fair price from me. And I

am the only one to decide if it is or not." He stood up again, still smiling for one last time at Andre. "I want Andre very much. You want your Timothy; you've told me so. We will have both."

Now he did look at Olaf. "Take off your clothes and prepare for your rings. I'm taking you to Montclair this afternoon. He's to have you for three days, precisely. I'm going to take you to him as a slave, Olaf; that is what you are whenever I put those rings in your hands.

"You will have three days to remember. Montclair is well known in our world. It won't bore you. It shouldn't make you feel so humbled in the way you seem to be. You will also value your Timothy all the more. You can, I'm sure, find ways to let him know just how much you've paid for him."

Harold turned to us. "Pull out, Timothy. The two of you kneel up. Watch how a man in my household prepares himself for service. It will instruct you; it will let you know what your life will become."

His face, which so often looked fatherly, so benevolent, had a different expression on it, one that seemed more harsh, more tyrannical, than I'd ever guessed it could be.

I felt my cock slip unwillingly out of Andre. Harold nodded to me, and I pulled off the condom, taking it carefully to throw it away. I came back to kneel beside Andre on the floor.

Olaf was undressing himself for the first time since I'd been with him. His own large hands undid the buttons that had always been handled by my teeth. I wanted to go over to him, to do this for him, as I was used to doing. But I could see that it wouldn't have been allowed. Harold was standing there, watching him; we were all viewing the transformation of my proud, muscular master.

Olaf's head hung down as though he were going through a transformation of his personality along with these physical actions. He hung his shirt over his chair. Then he kicked off his shoes. He undid his slacks and let them drop to the floor. He peeled off his socks next and stood wearing nothing but his briefs. I could see his fat cock, still heavy from his recent orgasm. He bent and pulled off the underwear. He stood there naked.

I watched carefully and saw what I'd expected, the proof that he was entering that world he'd told me about, the one where he was not my master but Harold's slave. His cock was lifting up with blood at his nakedness, at his submission.

He reached over and took the rings from the table where he'd left them. He put one each through his nipples. Then he lifted up his balls and found the hole that was in that most private part of his body, between his cock and his asshole. He wove the ring through there. The last ring went onto the head of his cock, just behind the slit at the very top of it.

He was transformed. He was now a ringed, nude slave, waiting for his service to be defined, ready to perfectly fulfill his master's every request.

"Your collar." Harold stood there and spoke quietly.

Olaf went to his dresser and opened a drawer I'd never been in. He retrieved a stunningly handsome neckpiece. It was made of gold, with images sculpted on it. I strained to see them and then to understand what they were. I remembered some from pictures I'd seen in books. They were Norse gods.

Olaf brought the collar to Harold and then knelt as though he were some Viking before his liege lord. His rings added to the air of barbarism. His head was bowed. His eyes were closed. The moment was religious and didn't seem to belong to our time and place. I saw Olaf's huge shaved body shudder when he felt the gold drop onto his shoulders and the hinged arc of metal close around his neck. There was a snap of a lock. Harold withdrew a key. He put it into his pocket.

"Walk behind me, Olaf. Prepare your mind for your master."

And then they left us in the room alone.

Andre was still there with me. He seemed shocked, unable to speak for a while. He finally stammered out, "What's going to happen?"

I was sitting there as calm as I'd ever been in my life. I didn't look at him, but studied the closed door through which the two masters had just left.

"It's obvious," I said, "that we're going to change owners. Aren't you happy?"

"Yes, of course I am. Harold's wonderful. He's a man like I've only dreamed of before. There's so much . . . range to what he can do, who he can be. I'm always on guard, always trying to please him. The sex is amazing. I'm very happy I'm going with him. But Olaf, what do you think of Olaf now?"

I stood up and went to where my master's clothes were lying on the floor. I took the slacks and shirt and hung them up. I put the shoes near the foot of the bed, where I'd remember to polish them. Then I went to where his white briefs were on the floor. I knelt down and smelled a hint of Olaf.

"This changes nothing. Nothing Montclair can do makes Olaf less than what he is: my master. Probably the master I'll have for the rest of my life." Then I bent down farther and picked up the briefs with my mouth. While Andre watched, I carried them that way back to my futon. I put them on the small pile of the others and used my teeth to rearrange my nighttime altar. I would only have this for a while. Harold had said that Olaf would be with Montclair for three days. I was already feeling a physical pain from the loneliness.

17

The End: The Beginning

They had to help Olaf when he came back to his room—our room. Peter and Jim were both holding him up. He seemed to be so exhausted and so stiff that he couldn't stand on his own, let alone walk.

His naked body was filthy with sweat, and there was already stubble growing from parts of it that were usually shaved. They left him on the bed, facedown. I could see that Peter had been part of all of it. His back was striped with new marks; his eyes showed nearly as much exhaustion as Olaf's.

Jim left Peter and me with my master without saying a word. I went and got the salves that Harold had given me, preparing for just this. I put them on the table by the bed and then went into the bathroom to soak some towels in hot water. Peter followed me.

"I've never been through anything like it. I've never seen anything like it." His voice had a faraway sound to it. "It was the most wonderful experience of my life."

"And of Olaf's?" I asked; my anger was obvious.

"He was the most astonishing part of all of it. There wasn't a thing he didn't do, a thing that Montclair asked that he didn't provide. I doubt I can ever be that strong, not like him, not in my mind and my body both."

I tried to hide the pride I felt by making myself busy with the towels. I carried them into the bedroom and immediately began to carefully wash off Olaf's body.

He smiled when he felt the warmth. "Timothy," he said quietly.

"Shhh, be quiet. Let me take care of you."

"Of course I will. You know I will." He smiled even more then, and his eyes closed.

I ran the first towel over his shoulders. Their enormous expanse was cut with raised red welts where a whip had made the same symmetrical, artfully applied marks on him as I'd seen on Peter another time. I moved the towel over his flesh, watching as the grime disappeared and the welts became even more obvious to my eyes. I got to his buttocks, those twin mounds of flesh that, while still harder than most men's, felt so soft after the feel of the developed muscles of his back.

I massaged them carefully. I ran the edge of the cotton into the cleft between his ass. He moaned pleasurably.

"That ass was well used," Peter said. "He spent most of his time with a plug up there and almost all the rest with Montclair's cock buried in it, and once even with mine."

"I don't want to know, Peter."

"Yes, you do. You do," Peter said. "Because you'll have to pay for every minute of it. It's part of your purchase price. Did you know that?"

"Yes. I was here when he was told."

"You're going to Norway."

"With Andre."

"What do you think, that he won't make you pay him back for what he went through?"

"I don't care." I was wiping the backs of Olaf's thighs now. Then I washed his calves and the bottom of his feet. When I was done with that, I put my arms under him, on his stomach. I coaxed him to roll over. He did it, his body stiff with pain when he made the movement.

I took up a new towel and began to wash his face. He liked the touch; he sighed again to let me know that.

"I don't know what he'll do about this," I said honestly. But in my mind there were images of rings being attached to my flesh, at my nipples, in my ball sac, on my cock. "It won't matter. I'm going to make him forget it all. I'm going to be too perfect for him to bother remembering."

"You make big promises," Peter said.

"Don't you do the same?" I was washing Olaf's flat, hard stomach now. "Don't you make promises to Montclair?"

"Of course I do. I mean them. I know you mean your own. This is what you wanted, isn't it? Your magician?"

I thought of Olaf and the way he'd looked when the collar was put on him. The memory of the barbaric Viking came back to me. I suddenly realized that the collar was gone, so were the rings. "Where's the metal? The things he wore?"

"Harold took them back. He pounded on Montclair's door at the exact minute the three days were up and demanded that Montclair release Olaf. He removed all the jewelry and ordered that we bring him back here."

I looked more closely and saw that the places where the rings had been attached were raw. The flesh around the holes had been put to harsh use. I imagined weights hanging from the rings or Montclair pulling them, tugging at them while Olaf screamed in pain.

"Your master crawled."

"Why tell me that now?" I was washing Olaf's thighs. "Do you expect me to think less of him?"

"No, not at all. I didn't bring it up for that. It was just so amazing. I saw what I might have looked like—what I might look like if I ever get to be like him. It was incredible."

I dried Olaf off then and went about rubbing the salve over his skin. He opened his eyes when he felt the cool lotion on him. "My Timothy," he said sleepily.

"Yes, sir."

I kept on massaging him, forgetting the idea of taking care of him and just being happy to be able to touch him so completely.

"I'm glad you're going to Norway, that you're not going to have to stay in the salon for your whole contract," Peter said.

I was startled. I nearly stopped my massage. . . . *Your whole contract.* The phrase seemed so strange, so alien. I hadn't thought in terms of my contract since the first night I'd been here in this room with Olaf. I'd only thought of my entire life.

And Andre? I wondered.

"Yes, Peter, I'm glad, too," I finally answered. I was at the foot of the bed, rubbing salve into the rough calluses on Olaf's feet. I'd massaged him there before, for hours at a time. I was getting hard, thinking of it, thinking of all the time I'd be doing it from now on.

The 747 was poised for takeoff. I listened to the jet's engines revving up. Then, after their power had been held back long enough to produce the necessary thrust, the plane began to race down the runway. It was so huge that I couldn't understand how it was able to fly. But like my muscular master, it defied its size and turned itself into something graceful.

The four of us were sitting in the first-class cabin. A steward offered drinks as soon as we were airborne. In this part of the plane, on a level above the rest of the passengers, the seats weren't arranged in repetitious rows; they were set up like small conversation areas. We had no one else near us.

Olaf ordered for us in one of the Scandinavian languages; I hadn't been able to tell them apart yet—Norwegian from Swedish. It didn't make any difference. I knew I'd take whatever he decided.

The steward returned with our drinks. I was handed a small glass of clear liquid. I took it and looked at it, trying to figure it out. "Aquavit," the steward said. "The gentleman thought you'd like to try something Scandinavian."

"Thank you; it's fine."

"The house is a few miles from Oslo, on the coast. There's a great deal of privacy, but we're able to get to the city very easily. The discipline in my home is more severe than Montclair's in some ways," Harold was telling Andre, "but in other, more ordinary ways, it's more relaxed. You'll not have to live in a prison; there are no cells for the servants."

"Are there others?" Andre asked.

"Yes," Harold answered, "but they won't be like you."

"Like me?"

"They won't be living in my own quarters. They're there simply for entertainment.

"I'll expect you to take up your studies again. It's not appropriate for you to not care for your education. I expect you'll learn Norwegian well enough in less than a year."

"This lack of discipline," Andre said quietly, "doesn't mean that I've—"

"You are not released from your contract. I simply find it more enjoyable to leave the stricter rules behind on occasion."

Andre looked directly at Olaf. "It must make it all the more difficult when they are called for."

"More difficult for you, perhaps," Harold said. "More interesting for me." The older man looked out the window as the North American coastline disappeared. "My pleasure is, you'll remember, what we're concerned with."

"I'm just thinking of the emotions that must be involved when someone has to move from freedom to slavery on his master's whim. I'm trying to imagine how it must feel." Andre's face wasn't showing any concern, though. I remembered his declarations about the swings of his passions and how much he'd wanted to feel that constantly. I could see him walking into a house from class at a university and finding himself confronted by his master holding a set of golden rings and a sculpted collar. . . .

"What are you thinking about?" Olaf asked me suddenly.

"About living in Norway." It was true, at least in a sense. I was really thinking about how very far this airplane was taking me from that place I'd once thought was home. I had wanted my life changed. I'd wanted to break with my past and its boredom and its emptiness. I'd accomplished that; certainly where I was going was as far away from my old life as it could possibly be. I was flying across the Atlantic, sitting beside my owner, with welts on my back and ass and legs that were only a few days newer than those on his. I'd paid for my trip once Olaf had regained his strength. It'd been a wonderful night, one I'd wanted to give him.

Olaf had told me that I could forget Montclair and that I was never to think that I had any responsibility for the three days he'd spent there. He had, he'd said, given himself to Harold for whatever Harold wanted for those certain number of days in their contract. He accepted Harold's decision, never holding it against him and never bringing up the subject with the older man.

But I couldn't live with the idea that my master had gone through so much and I hadn't. I'd come to Olaf on my hands and knees the first day he seemed to have his strength back, carrying a riding crop in my mouth. I'd begged him to beat me and to do it as hard as he could, as though it were the most deserved punishment of all. I wanted that from him. I wanted to go through that for him.

I was still amazed and happy that he'd let me give it to him, ask him to accept it from me, instead of simply taking it himself.

"Don't listen too carefully to what Harold's telling Andre," Olaf continued. He was better now, healed from this trial with Montclair after a few days in a hotel room in New York. He seemed happy. He had me. He had his business agreement with Montclair. And more, I bet. "I don't subscribe to the same rules he has."

"It doesn't matter," I said honestly. I looked around the cabin and wished the rest of the passengers and the crew were gone. I wanted to get on my knees with my head between Olaf's legs, that place I'd learned to love so much.

"I think I'll build you a small house of your own," Olaf was saying almost dreamily. "I'll put it behind the big house. Not a cell but someplace where you and I can build some interesting . . . equipment. We'll need a more sophisticated space to work out in as well. You need much more exercise for your body."

"Enough to make it worth shaving my hair?" We weren't even an hour into our journey and my cock was already hard, my underwear wet.

Olaf put a hand on top of my thigh; he at least didn't care about the people around us. "Yes, I'm sure we'll do that soon enough."

"And the rings?" I finally took the drink I'd been served, and as I'd seen Olaf do, I drank it all at once, happy to have the sudden burning sensation in my throat, anything to take my mind off what I'd just said.

"The rings have nothing to do with the body. They need more justification. They need proof of something more powerful than just sheer force."

I closed my eyes, and no matter what else I tried to think of, the only sensation I was aware of was the hand on my thigh. It was kneading my flesh, hard, just hard enough that both Olaf and I knew there was that between us. I played back his words and, not opening my eyes, just said, "Yes, master."